Ella and the Soulless

Andrew S. French

Neonoir Books

Copyright © 2025 by A. S. French

All rights reserved.

No part of this book may be reproduced in any form or by any electronic or mechanical means, including information storage and retrieval systems, without written permission from the author, except for the use of brief quotations in a book review.

This is a work of fiction. Names, characters, places, events, businesses, locales and incidents are either the products of the author's imagination or used in a fictitious manner. Any resemblance to actual persons, living or dead, or actual events is purely coincidental.

Also by Andrew S. French

The Arcane Supernatural Thriller Series

The Arcane

The Arcane Identity

The Arcane Quest

The Arcane Ultimatum

The Ella Finn Fantasy Series

Ella and the Elementals

Ella and the Multiverse

Ella and the Monsters

Ella and the Dreamers

Supernatural Short Stories

Dead Souls

Dead Souls II

Dead Souls III

The Shadow

Science Fiction

The Time Traveller's Murder

The Mercy Sleep

Bodies

Another Girl, Another Planet

The Thief of Time Trilogy

The Queens of Heaven

The Queens of Time

The Queens of Space

Writing as A. S. French
Crime Fiction and Thrillers

The Astrid Snow series

Don't Fear the Reaper

The Killing Moon

Lost in America

Gone to Texas

The Final Girl

Snowstorm: An Astrid Snow Collection

Astrid Snow: The Collection

The Detective Jen Flowers series

The Hashtag Killer

Serial Killer

Night Killer

The Killer Inside Them

Inspector Flowers Collection: Books 1-4

Northern Crime Fiction

Where The Bodies Are Buried

Bodies of Evidence

The Lulu Chase Mysteries

The Strange Case of Madam X

Teesside Crime Series

No More Heroes

The Ophelia Red series

Book one: Ophelia Red

Crime Short Stories

Call Me: An Astrid Snow Short Story

Crime Stories: A Collection

Shirley Holmes Cosy Mysteries

A Scandal in Bohemia-on-Sea

Chapter 1

The Island

Ella Finn fell out of a tree on her fourteenth birthday.

It was a long fall, only ended by a thick pile of leaves. The ground was so hard it sent a surge of electricity through her legs, around her waist, and up to her shoulders. She rolled over, with dirt in her nose and tasting wet mud. The forest buzzed with life - the gentle rustling of leaves in the breeze, the distant calls of exotic birds, and the soft scurrying of small creatures in the underbrush. Ella's fingers dug into the spongy moss beneath her, its cool dampness pressing against her skin.

'Are you okay, Ella?'

She blinked through the dizziness. 'I might have hurt myself, Agrius.'

The centaur trotted forward. 'It looks like you may have broken your hip, my friend.'

She winced as she touched the damage. 'How can you tell from up there?'

'Hercules did the same thing once, and I took him to the

physician. He'd been in a fight and not climbing a tree. What were you doing up there?'

The buzz in her legs increased. 'I was looking for the Golden Apple.'

Agrius shook his head, his long mane swishing in the dappled sunlight filtering through the canopy. 'There are no Golden Apples on this island, Ella. The dragon Ladon guards the Golden Apple tree, and as far as I'm aware, he's still trapped in the Elemental world.' He reached towards her. 'Now take my hand and let my Light heal you.'

She twisted through the pain and lifted one hand to him. His grip was firm but gentle, and his skin was warm. Then it got warmer, euphoria sweeping through her. This was his Light travelling into her, transforming Ella into something more than she was as it spread down to her hip and repaired it. It was as if she'd taken a comforting bath, and the water softened her skin. The Light felt like liquid sunshine coursing through her veins, a tingling warmth that surged from her fingertips to her toes. It tasted like honey on her tongue and smelled like a summer breeze. As it worked its magic, Ella heard a faint musical hum.

She released his hand after a minute, pushing up and smiling. 'Thank you, Agrius.'

'Should I take you back to the camp, Ella?'

His question surprised her. Centaurs carried nothing on their backs, not that she'd met any others apart from him. She was about to refuse his offer until the stabbing electricity returned to her hip when she moved her leg.

She held out her hand. 'That's kind of you, Agrius, thank you.' He hoisted her up. There was nothing to hold on to, so she leaned forward next to his head. 'But don't you dare tell any of the others what happened to me.'

He laughed as he trotted away. 'As if I would, my young friend.'

As they moved through the forest, Ella marvelled at the beauty of their surroundings. The trees were unlike any she'd seen, with bark that shimmered in iridescent hues and leaves that seemed to whisper secrets as they rustled in the breeze. Strange, luminous fungi dotted the ground, casting a soft, ethereal glow in the shadowy undergrowth. A whispering mist clung to the grass, nipping at Agrius's legs. The scent of unfamiliar flowers, their intoxicating and alien fragrances, lingered everywhere. Ella heard the distant sound of water, its gentle burbling a soothing counterpoint to the occasional cries of unseen creatures in the canopy above.

As they neared the camp, the forest thinned out, giving way to a tiny clearing. The sudden brightness made her squint, her eyes adjusting to the change in the light. The air was different, carrying the scent of wood smoke and cooking food, mingling with the forest's natural fragrance.

They returned to a cluster of tents Seraphina had conjured up when she had Light to spare. Agrius helped Ella down. She grimaced as the pain burst through her hip, and she tried to keep her discomfort from her parents. But she couldn't kid her mother.

'What happened, Ella?' Gemma Finn said as she ran to her daughter.

Ella touched her waist to quell the shiver running through her. 'It's nothing, Mum. I fell over, that's all.' Agrius shook his head as he trotted away. 'Where's Dad?'

'He's at the river, helping the others collect water.'

Ella thought of them: Seraphina, the witch who'd brought them to the island and was using all of her Elemental power to keep it hidden from the human world -

especially the Institute, the clandestine British government organisation created to hunt and imprison Elementals. They'd been enemies once, Ella and Seraphina, but now they were united against the Institute.

In addition, they received help from Veronica Venus, a former Institute agent who had betrayed her employers. Venus had fled from the Institute, bringing her twenty-year-old daughter Catherine after Seraphina had used her Light to remove Catherine from her coma.

Also helping them to escape from the north of England and an underground Institute prison was Sigrun the Valkyrie, now known as Barbara.

'A new name for a new life,' the Valkyrie had announced on their arrival.

Ella had liked her the minute they'd met, feeling a sistership with the warrior even before she aided their flight to the island.

And that flight wouldn't have happened without Seraphina's friend, Gisela, the dragon. The witch and the dragon communicated in a language only they understood, though Seraphina had promised she'd teach it to Ella once they were safe. Gisela's ability to turn invisible was a rare Elemental power.

When they reached the island, Seraphina had instructed Gisela to take them to the camp, where Ella met four Elementals Seraphina had rescued from an Institute prison: Callisto, the female bear; Kitty Stardust, the six-foot-tall talking cat who walked on two legs; Delf the Elf, and Peg Powler, a water spirit.

Agrius had lived on the island for a while. 'My escape and prison,' he'd said.

It had been a week since Seraphina had arranged for the group to shelter on the island, and they'd spent most of that time coming to terms with their current situation. For the Elementals, it was recognising they were being hunted; for the humans, it was the realisation they could never return to their former lives. Ella had adapted quickly, but she was worried about her parents. They'd only recently discovered that Elementals and portals to other worlds existed, and she was concerned their scientific minds might bend or break under the revelation. However, this wasn't all new to them since she'd wiped the same information from their memories over a year ago – which they were unaware of.

The guilt of that haunted her.

She grabbed her mother's hand. 'Let's see what they're doing.'

They strode towards the river. They stepped between the trees, and Ella glanced at the colourful flowers around them, inhaling all the different scents. She tried to hide her limp, but it was impossible.

'Are you sure you're okay, Ella?' Gemma Finn couldn't disguise her concern.

Ella nodded, forcing a smile. 'I'm fine, Mum. Just a bit sore from the fall.'

As they walked, Ella's mind wandered to the events that had led them to this strange, magical island. The past two years had been a whirlwind of discovery, danger, and transformation. She remembered the first time she'd encountered an Elemental, the fear and wonder that had coursed through her. Now, surrounded by these mystic beings, she felt a sense of belonging she'd never experienced before.

The forest path widened, and the sound of running water grew louder. Soon, they emerged onto the banks of a crystal-clear river cutting through the island. The liquid sparkled in the sunlight, its surface broken by the occasional jump of a fish or the ripples caused by the gentle current.

On the riverbank, Ella saw her father, Andrew, working alongside other members of their eclectic group. He was knee-deep in the water, his trousers rolled up to his thighs, filling a large container. Beside him, Barbara stood guard, studying the surrounding forest for any sign of danger. Her golden armour gleamed in the sunlight, contrasting the island's lush green landscape.

Kitty Stardust, the talking humanoid cat, sat perched on a rock, her fur a shimmering array of colours that shifted and changed with the light. She was deep in conversation with Delf the Elf, who used his magic to purify the water as they collected it.

'Dad!' Ella shouted, waving to get his attention.

Andrew looked up, a broad smile spreading across his face as he saw his daughter and wife approaching. He returned to the shore, water streaming from his clothes.

'Happy birthday, sweetheart,' he said, embracing her in a wet hug. 'I was hoping to surprise you, but you found us.'

She hugged him back, inhaling her father's familiar scent and the fresh smell of the river. 'Thanks, Dad. What are you doing?'

'We're collecting and purifying water for the camp,' Andrew explained, gesturing to the containers lined up on the shore. 'Delf's magic makes it safer to drink, and we're hoping to store enough to last us a while.'

Ella noticed Peg Powler, the water spirit, emerge from the river. Her form was fluid and ethereal. Droplets clung to her translucent skin, refracting the sunlight into tiny rainbows. When she spoke, her voice was like the gentle babbling of a brook.

'Young Ella,' Peg said, her words somehow both whisper-soft and crystal clear. 'Many happy returns on your day of birth. The river sings songs of celebration for you.'

Warmth spread through Ella. 'Thank you, Peg. That's very kind of you.'

She spoke to her mother. 'Where are Veronica and Catherine?'

'In their tent,' Gemma Finn replied. 'Catherine is still suffering from the after-effects of her coma.'

Ella nodded, knowing Veronica hadn't revealed much about their new, enforced life to her daughter. As the group continued their work, she helped where she could, trying to ignore the lingering ache in her hip. The sun climbed higher in the sky, its heat tempered by the cool breeze from the river. The occasional splash of water or rustle of leaves punctuated the laughter and conversation.

Then it all changed.

A roar echoed through the forest, causing everybody to freeze. Ella's heart raced as she recognised the sound — Callisto, the bear Elemental. But this wasn't Callisto's usual gentle rumble. This was a cry of alarm.

Barbara was the first to react, her warrior instincts kicking in. 'Everyone, back to the camp. Now!' she commanded, her voice brooking no argument.

Ella's mind buzzed with possibilities as they hurried along the path. Had the Institute found them? Was there some other danger on the island they hadn't discovered yet? The pain in her hip was forgotten as she ran alongside her parents, fear and adrenaline propelling her.

They burst into the clearing where their tents were, and Ella gasped at the sight. Callisto stood at the edge of the camp, her massive form tense and ready for action. But it wasn't an enemy she faced, but Seraphina.

Seraphina looked different - dishevelled, her hair wild, and her clothes torn. But her eyes caught Ella's attention — they glowed with an intense, wraithlike light.

'Seraphina?' Ella asked, taking a step forward. 'What's wrong?'

The witch turned to them, and Ella shivered. Seraphina's voice, when she spoke, was overlaid with another, deeper tone that seemed to echo from somewhere far away.

'Ella Finn,' Seraphina said, her glowing eyes fixed on the young girl. 'The veil between worlds is thinning. The Soulless are coming, bringing a darkness that threatens to consume everything. You must be ready.'

The air thickened, heavy with an unseen power. Ella tasted something metallic on her tongue, like the aftermath of a lightning strike. The hairs on her arms stood on end, and she felt a familiar tingling in her fingertips – her connection to the Light responding to the surge of magical energy.

Gemma and Andrew moved closer to their daughter while Barbara stepped forward, her hand on her sword. Kitty Stardust's fur sprang upwards, crackling with static electricity, while Delf muttered quiet incantations, his hands weaving intricate patterns in the air.

'What do you mean, Seraphina?' Ella asked, her voice trembling. 'What darkness? Who are The Soulless? And how am I supposed to be ready?'

Seraphina staggered forward, and Ella noticed beads of sweat on the witch's forehead. Whatever was happening to her was taking a toll.

'The Book of All Life,' Seraphina gasped. 'You must master it, Ella. It's the key to everything. The balance between our world and the Elemental realm is shifting, and you are the fulcrum upon which it all turns.'

As soon as it had come, the strange energy dissipated. Seraphina's eyes returned to normal, and she swayed on her feet before collapsing. Callisto sprang forward, catching the witch before she hit the earth.

For a moment, no one moved. The only sound was the gentle rustle of leaves and Seraphina's laboured breathing. Then, as if a spell had been broken, everyone burst into action.

Andrew and Gemma rushed to Seraphina's side, their scientific training kicking in as they checked her vital signs. Barbara issued orders and organised a perimeter watch in case whatever had affected Seraphina was part of a larger threat. Kitty Stardust and Delf huddled together, speaking in hushed, worried tones.

Ella stood rooted to the spot, her mind reeling from Seraphina's words. The Book of All Life, the powerful artefact that had started her on this journey and opened her life to the world of Elementals and magic - she'd used it before, but mastering it? The thought was both exhilarating and terrifying.

Ella felt a gentle touch on her shoulder as the others bustled around her. She turned to see Agrius, the centaur's kind eyes filled with concern.

'Are you okay, young one?' he asked.

Ella took a deep breath, trying to steady herself. 'I... I don't know. Everything's happening so fast. What did Seraphina mean? What am I supposed to do?'

Agrius smiled, his hand warm and reassuring on her shoulder. 'The path of a hero is never clear, Ella. But you have faced challenges before and have always risen to meet them. Whatever comes, you do not face it alone.'

She nodded, grateful for the centaur's words. She gazed at the strange creatures that had become her friends and allies. Humans and Elementals working together in the face

of an unknown threat. And at the centre of it all was her –
Ella Finn, no longer just a girl but a bridge between worlds.

As the sun set, painting the sky in brilliant hues of
orange and pink, she went to her tent. The Book of All Life
lay tucked in a box. Its cover seemed to pulse with an inner
light, as if responding to the heightened energies around it.
She placed her hand on it, seeing the images of Elementals
on the cover shimmer and change.

And the pain in her hip vanished.

Chapter 2

Legends and Revelations

They gathered around a blistering fire as night fell. Everyone was there, apart from Catherine Venus, resting in the tent she shared with her mother. The flames cast flickering shadows across their faces, highlighting their worries and doubts. Still weak from her earlier trauma, Seraphina sat propped against a tree, distant and unfocused. Her ordeal had unsettled them all.

Ella hugged her knees to her chest, the warmth of the fire doing little to dispel the chill in her bones. Her parents were on either side of her, their presence comforting in the swirling uncertainty.

Barbara stood at the firelight's edge, her gaze sweeping the darkness beyond. The metallic sheen of her armour reflected the dancing flames, giving her an otherworldly appearance.

Agrius cleared his throat. 'Perhaps,' he suggested, 'it would be helpful to share what we know. This circle has much wisdom from many different realms and experiences.'

Her multi-coloured fur shimmering in the firelight, Kitty Stardust nodded in agreement. 'Yes, I think that's a splendid idea. After all, knowledge is power, and it seems we'll need all we can muster.'

Gemma leaned forward, the sparkle in her eyes matching the flickering flames. 'I'd love to hear more about you all.' Her gaze moved from Kitty to Callisto, then to Delf and Peg. 'To get to know you better.'

The massive bear Elemental shifted her weight, the ground trembling beneath her. When she spoke, her voice was a low, rumbling growl that seemed to vibrate in Ella's chest.

'I am Callisto - daughter of Lycaon - a woman who once roamed the mountains and forests with Artemis, my life bound by the hunt and the stars. I was not always a bear, not this twisted form of fur and claws. I was once a nymph, a follower of Artemis, the goddess of the moon and the wilderness. My tale is ancient, tangled in love, betrayal, and punishment—set into motion by the gods and shaped by their cruel whims.

'It started with Zeus. His eyes alighted upon me as it has upon countless others, and despite my loyalty to Artemis and my vow to remain chaste, he pursued me. His deception was as deep as his desires, and he tricked me in the form of Artemis. What followed shattered my world. When the truth was revealed, the gods' wrath fell on me, not him. In her rage and jealousy, Hera saw not her husband's betrayal but my perceived duplicity. Her vengeance was swift and unmerciful. I was transformed, my human form stripped away and replaced with that of a bear.

'For years, I roamed the wilds as a beast, trapped in the body of a creature I once hunted. I felt the loss of my identity like a dagger through my heart—every glance at the reflection in the water was a reminder of what I once was. My son, Arcas, was taken from me and raised without knowledge of his true mother. I was alone, separated from the life I once knew, haunted by the memory of the woman I had been. The gods stole everything from me except for one thing—my will to survive.

'It was that will which carried me through the years, the isolation of my curse, and even the eventual reconciliation with Arcas. When we finally met again, he did not know me. How could he? He saw only a bear, and when he raised his spear against me, I did not defend myself. I had accepted my fate.

'But the gods intervened once more. Zeus took pity on us in a rare act of remorse or guilt. He cast me and my son into the stars, transforming us into the constellations Ursa Major and Ursa Minor. It was not forgiveness—it was another prison, one made of the heavens themselves.

'I thought my story had ended there, that I would spend eternity in the sky, watching the world change below while I remained fixed and forgotten. But the universe has strange ways of twisting fate. One day, the stars shimmered around me, and the darkness cracked wide open, starlight blinding me as I fell. Everything was a blur, my mind a hive of confusion, until I hit the ground. It was as if gravity had reclaimed me, yanking me back to Earth into a place that had long since moved on without me.

'My return was not a triumphant one. I was not the same Callisto who had been a follower of Artemis, nor was I the creature that had been transformed into a bear. I was something in between, a being torn between worlds. The Institute captured me as soon as I arrived, my confusion stopping me from fighting back.

'Their methods were cruel. They experimented on me, probing the connection between my old form and my bear form, attempting to unlock the secrets of my transformation.

They believed that if they could understand what made me a bear and what made me a constellation, they could use that knowledge to control others like me to create their twisted versions of the myths.

'But I never broke. I endured their tests, their cages, and their torment. I had survived the wrath of Hera and the touch of Zeus—what were the petty cruelties of humans compared to that? Yet, even in captivity, I was aware of the world beyond my cell. I heard whispers of the Institute's enemies, of those who sought to destroy them and free those of us they held. Through these whispers, I learned of Ella, Seraphina, and the others fighting against the Institute's dark reach.

'When the chance for escape came, I took it. With Seraphina's help, I broke free of their prison, returning to the wilds, but I did not return to the life I had before. How could I? The world had changed, and so had I. I was no longer a bear, no longer just a constellation in the sky. I was Callisto, a woman forged by the gods and reforged by human cruelty.

'The Institute will fall, and when it does, I will be free— not because the gods willed it, but because I fought for it.'

Silence settled over everyone, Callisto's words heavy in everybody's hearts as she peered into the sky.

'Do you know what happened to your son, to Arcas?' Ella asked.

Callisto shook her head. 'The Elemental realm is infinite. It's more vast than you can imagine, a place where nature is alive and conscious. Arcas could be anywhere.'

Nobody wanted to say the unthinkable, that the Institute may have captured Arcas.

'The Greek gods are real?' Andrew Finn said.

Callisto's eyes, reflecting the firelight, seemed to hold

countless ancient secrets. 'Real and spiteful, but there is also great beauty in the Elemental world. In my part of the realm, vast forests stretch as far as the eye can see. Trees taller than mountains, their branches intertwining to create entire ecosystems in the sky. The ground beneath your feet pulses with life, and every rock, every stream, every gust of wind has a spirit of its own.'

Kitty Stardust chimed in, her tail swishing back and forth. 'Oh, but it's not all wilderness, dear. There are cities too, though perhaps not like the ones the humans are used to.' She glanced at Veronica, and her whiskers twitched in amusement. 'Imagine buildings that grow and change with the seasons, streets that rearrange themselves according to the whims of their inhabitants. In my home, the City of Endless Twilight, the sky is always the colour of sunset, and the air tastes like your favourite dessert. Sometimes, it's warm cinnamon, like a fresh-baked apple pie; other times, it's cool, like lemon sorbet on a summer day. Everyone there feels a little lighter, as if the sweetness in the air lifts your soul and keeps your spirit high. It's home, and trust me, there's nowhere like it.'

All eyes were fixed on her.

'I wasn't always a walking, talking cat. I had your run-of-the-mill start, chasing mice and lounging in sunbeams like any other feline. But something about me was different from the beginning. Deep inside, I had a spark, a feeling I didn't belong to the ordinary world of barns, alleys, or comfy couches. I wasn't destined to be someone's pet or stay confined by the mundane. I craved more. Then I found it, or it found me—I'm still unsure which came first.

'I stumbled into The City of Endless Twilight, or maybe it stumbled into me. It's a place that exists between worlds, and sometimes, if you're lucky or strange enough, you'll slip through the cracks and find yourself there. One minute, I was chasing fireflies in a field, and the next, the world shimmered around me, like sunlight glinting off water, and I was somewhere else.

'The City is a marvel. The streets are cobbled with stone that hums beneath your feet, as if the earth is alive, breathing in sync with you. The buildings are a riot of colour, twisting upward into spirals, towers, and bridges that defy gravity. And the sky is forever painted in shades of violet, orange, pink, and gold, like the longest, most beautiful sunset you've ever seen. It's never day or night, just always in between. The air, thick with magic, wraps around you, and the scent, that sugary sweetness, lingers in every breath. There's no sun, no stars, only an endless twilight that stretches on and on.

'Those who live there, well, they're as unique as the city itself. Some are like me, creatures given a second chance, a new life filled with possibilities. Others are old souls, ancient beings wandering for aeons, keeping secrets only the twilight knows. But there's one thing we all have in common—we're all a little bit magical.

'My transformation happened gradually. The longer I lived in the city, the more I sensed it reshaping me inside and out. First, I learned to walk on two legs. It wasn't conscious; it felt natural, like I'd always been meant to stand upright. And I grew tall. Next came the voice. Initially, it was just meowing with more intention, but eventually, words spilt out. Real words and thoughts shaped into sounds that others could understand. It felt like I was unlocking a part of myself that had always been there, waiting to be set free.

'Life in The City of Endless Twilight was, in a word, perfect. I'd wander through the streets, mingling with others, swapping stories, and learning magic—yes, magic. Everyone in the city has some level of power, whether or not they know it, and I was no exception. I could manipulate light, bend it around me to cloak myself in shadows or make the twilight shine brighter. I could slip through the cracks of the city, moving between places in the blink of an eye. It was a good life, and I'd have stayed there forever if it weren't for them—the Institute.'

Her fur bristled as she continued.

'The Institute found its way to the City, sniffing out magic wherever it hides, searching for anomalies, creeping through portals. They're relentless, cold, and clinical. They don't care about the beauty of the worlds they invade. They only care about control, power, and ways to bend it to their will. I didn't know they were watching me, not at first. They have their ways, slipping into places they don't belong, sending scouts, setting traps. They caught wind of me. To them, I was just another specimen, something to study and break.

'It happened at night, or what passes for night in the City. I was wandering the rooftops, watching the endless twilight swirl above, feeling the hum of the cobblestones below. I should have sensed something was wrong, but the City, for all its wonders, can lull you into a false sense of security.

'The invaders hit me with something, some net or cage, but it wasn't physical. It was made of pure energy, a force that drained the light from around me and sucked the magic right out of the air. I tried to fight and disappear into the shadows, but the City didn't respond. The twilight, which had always protected me, felt distant, unreachable. They dragged me out of my home, out of the City, through one of their damned portals, and into their sterile, cold world.

'The Institute was everything the City wasn't. If my home was alive, filled with warmth, colour, and magic, the Institute was dead, grey, and suffocating. They threw me into a cell and treated me like some lab experiment. They didn't understand what they had. They thought they could break me down, strip away the magic, and figure out what made me unique. But here's the thing—they didn't realise that my magic wasn't something they could dissect. It wasn't something you could bottle up or extract like a chemical compound. It was a part of me, woven into every fibre. You can't separate me from my magic any more than you can separate the twilight from the City.

'They tried, though. Oh, did they try. The tests, the experiments, the endless poking and prodding.' She raised her paws, and Ella saw the wounds. 'They cut pieces from me, but I held on. I clung to the memory of the City—the taste of the air, the hum of the streets, the glow of the eternal sunset. They couldn't take that from me. And in the end, that connection, that tie to my home, kept me alive.'

She glanced at Seraphina.

'I don't know how long I was trapped in that sterile hell, but one day, the opportunity came – my saviour arrived. I miss the City of Endless Twilight every day. I miss how the sky looked like a painting and the air tasted like home. But I know I can't go back, not yet. Not until the Institute is gone or the people they've hurt are free. Not until my friends are safe.'

Ella gazed at Kitty, picturing her as a regular cat before her strange and terrifying adventures. She touched Kitty's arm. 'I'm glad you're with us.' She looked at all their faces. 'I'm happy to have you all as friends.'

Her parents nodded before Gemma Finn spoke, gripping her husband's hand.

'And we appreciate everything you've all done for Ella and us. But if this is resurrecting difficult experiences, maybe we should get some rest.'

But nobody wanted to leave.

'All that we are is stories,' Seraphina said. 'And these are theirs.'

Chapter 3

Elementals

A wistful expression crossed Delf the Elf's face. 'I want to talk. The magic in our world is as natural as breathing. It flows through everything and everyone. Even the smallest child can perform feats that would be miraculous here.' He waved his hand, and the fire turned a brilliant blue, its flames taking the shape of dancing figures.

Ella gasped in wonder, reaching out to feel the heat. It was cool to the touch, more like silk than flame. 'Amazing!'

Delf continued. 'My home is a place that most people can't even comprehend. Imagine a world where the elements breathe, where fire, water, air, and earth are not just forces of nature but living, conscious things that we, the elves, are deeply connected to. Each of us has a bond with one of the elements. For me, it's fire. I feel its pulse, its rhythm; I speak to it, and it listens. It flows through my veins, not just metaphorically, but in the essence of who I am.

'My family—my parents, siblings, and the rest of the clan—live deep in the heart of the Elemental realm. We're part of an ancient line of elves, protectors of the fires that flow through our world and the threads that connect it to other realms. My mother, a healer, and my father, a guardian of fire, taught me everything I know. From the time I was old enough to understand, I learned to listen to its beat, feel the balance in the flames, and protect it. That's what we elves do: we maintain the balance, not just in our world, but across many. There are countless realms, all interconnected, and if the balance in one is upset, it can ripple across the rest.

'That's why I was out there, beyond the Elemental realm, travelling between worlds. It was my duty, and I accepted it with pride. There were signs that something was wrong—portals between realms were opening up randomly, things that shouldn't have slipped through. I was tracking the disturbances, trying to figure out what was causing them and how to stop them. My journey took me to strange locations, human realms, faerie lands, and places where the air felt off. But nothing compared to the danger I found when I crossed paths with the Institute.

'I should've sensed them before they got close. I should've known something was wrong, but the human realms were so chaotic that I couldn't feel them coming. They were watching, waiting. I was an anomaly, another specimen they wanted to study, dissect, and understand. To them, I wasn't an elf trying to protect the realms; I was an opportunity, a rare creature out of place.

'They struck when I was vulnerable. The air was thick with the residue of the magic I'd used, and my connection to fire was weak. They came at me with their technology— cold, mechanical, devoid of any connection to the elements, to nature. It was alien to me but efficient. I fought, of course. I'm not just some scholar who studies the balance of the elements; I'm a protector. But their machines neutralised magic to trap beings like me in cages where even the elements couldn't reach us.

'They called it a containment field. To me, it felt like being cut off from my soul. Imagine being plunged into a void where you can't feel anything—not the fire, air, or even the pulse of life surrounding you. That's what they did to me. They took me from the Elemental realm, from the connection I have with everything, and imprisoned me in their cold, lifeless facility. They threw me into a cell made of materials I didn't understand, things that deadened my senses and blocked out my connection to fire. I was trapped, cut off from everything that made me who I am.

'At first, I thought they'd kill me. Or worse, dissect me like some experiment. They didn't, though. Not immediately. They wanted to know what I was and how I worked. They tried to figure out how an elf from the Elemental realm could exist in their world. The Institute is obsessed with magic, with creatures from other realms, but they don't understand it. They believe they can harness, control, and use it for their own purposes. They think they can bend it to their will if they study it enough.

'They questioned me. For days, weeks—maybe even longer. It's hard to tell how much time passed in that place. It was always the same sterile, cold environment: no windows, no light from the sun, no water. I couldn't feel the elements. I couldn't connect with anything. The questions were endless: "Where are you from?" "How do you control the elements?" "How can we do it too?"

'I didn't answer, of course. Not at first. But isolation does things to you. You weaken when you're cut off from everything you know, everything that makes you who you are. It was the first time in my life I'd ever felt fear like that, a deep, gnawing fear that I would never escape, never see my family again. The thought of my parents, siblings, and clan kept me going. I refused to give in to the Institute and let them break me because I had to get back. I had to return to my family and the Elemental realm. They needed me. The balance needed me.

'One day, something changed. There was a disturbance in the facility—a breakout, maybe. I'm unsure what caused it, but the alarms blared, and the containment field around my cell flickered. It was the first time I'd felt the faintest whisper of fire since I'd been captured. And then I saw her – Seraphina.'

He smiled at her.

'Seraphina rescued me and brought me here, in this world that isn't mine, cut off from my family and realm. I can feel the pull of the Elemental realm every day, like a distant song calling me home. All I want is to return to my family. My mother, my father—they don't even know if I'm alive. For all they know, I'm lost, another casualty of the endless fight to maintain balance between the realms. But I can't return to them until I've dealt with the Institute. If I lead them to the Elemental realm, they'll do to my world what they've done to so many others—strip it of its magic, cage its inhabitants, and turn it into something cold and dead.

'The Institute thinks they're unstoppable, that they can take whatever they want from any world and use it for their own gain. But they're wrong. They've made a mistake in underestimating us, in underestimating me. I may be far from home, but the fire still flows in my veins, and as long as it does, I'll keep fighting.

'I have to stop them. *We* have to stop them.'

Next, Peg Powler spoke. Her voice was like the gentle

lapping of waves on a shore. 'I'm a water spirit from the River Tees in the north of England. Deep below the water is a portal into the Elemental Realm. I'm not the spirit you'd find in your fairy tales or legends—I don't sit around singing to sailors or handing out wishes. No, I'm part of the river, born from the rushing waters and flowing currents that have shaped the land for centuries. My essence is tied to the river, to the life that pulses through it, and I've spent my life protecting it and all the creatures that depend on it. But that was before everything changed - before the Institute.

'You see, I wasn't always this...restless. For centuries, I was content in my domain. The Tees is my home, my sanctuary, and I could feel every ripple, every drop of rain that fed it. The water is part of me, and I'm part of it. People are not far off when they talk about the river being alive. We water spirits have been guardians of the waterways for as long as anyone can remember. My job was simple: keep the river clean, keep the balance of nature intact, and if humans stepped too far into the river's domain, well, I had ways of dealing with that.

'They used to tell stories about me back in the day. Peg Powler, the river witch who'd drag you under if you got too close to the water's edge. Mothers would warn their children not to play near the riverbanks, or Peg would snatch them. Those tales weren't true, of course. I harmed no one who didn't deserve it. But humans can be careless with nature, and sometimes, they need a reminder of the power that runs beneath the surface of things.

'My power comes from the water. I can shape it, bend it to my will, summon waves and currents, create mist and fog to hide in. I can even walk on the water's surface when I choose to, though I prefer to remain beneath it, where I'm strongest. My hair—green as the river weeds that grow along the banks—flows like water, and my skin has always shone as if I've just emerged from the depths. Some call it beauty. I call it home.

'For centuries, I did my duty. I kept to the Tees, guarding it, nurturing it. The river was my life, and I never imagined leaving it. Then, things changed. The balance of the natural world shifted, human pollution poisoning everything and weakening the barriers between worlds. Portals were opening in places they shouldn't—tearing through the fabric of reality. At first, it was small. Ripples in the water that didn't belong, strange things washing up on the riverbanks. Soon, the disruptions grew. I knew something was wrong.

'I wasn't the only one who felt it, either. Spirits, Elementals, and creatures from all over noticed. Something was causing these disturbances, and it was spreading. It wasn't just the Tees that was affected; other rivers, other bodies of water were feeling the strain, too. Pollution was everywhere, infecting and corrupting everything. The natural balance was breaking, and whatever was responsible was dangerous. I tried to investigate and trace the source of the disturbances, but that's when I crossed paths with the Institute.

'I didn't know what they were at first. Just strange humans poking around the riverbanks with their machines and their gadgets. They didn't seem to belong but weren't scared of the water either. They weren't like the usual fools who think they can conquer nature. No, these people knew what they were doing. They were looking for something—or rather, someone.

'I remember the day they captured me like it was yesterday. I was out on the river, checking a part of the bank where the water had been acting strangely. It was a foggy morning, the kind I love—the air thick with mist, the water cool against my skin. I should've sensed them before they got close, but the mist played tricks on me. By the time I realised what was happening, it was too late.

'They came at me with nets—machines that could cut through the water like it wasn't there. I tried to fight back, to summon the waves and currents to protect me, but their technology was unlike anything I'd seen. It wasn't just metal and wires. It was infused with something—magic or energy that disrupted my connection to the water. For the first time, I couldn't control the river.

'They dragged me from the water, bound me in restraints that sapped my strength, and threw me into a cold, metal cage. I remember the feeling of the air drying on my skin, the water slipping away, and I felt powerless for the first time. I don't know how long they kept me in that cage, but it felt like an eternity. They transported me to one of their facilities—a sterile, lifeless place that made my skin crawl. There was no water, no natural light, nothing I could connect to. They wanted to study me, to understand what I was and how I worked. To them, I was just another specimen to dissect, another puzzle to solve.

'They questioned me endlessly. Asked about my powers, about the river, about the portals. They wanted to know how I could manipulate the water, how I could control it. But I didn't give them what they wanted. I didn't tell them that my power came from the river and my deep connection with the natural world. I didn't tell them that without the water, I was nothing. They wouldn't understand. They were trying to break me, but I held on. I had to.

'While trapped in their facility, I learned more about the Institute. They weren't just interested in water spirits like me. They were after all kinds of magical creatures, beings from different realms and elements. They wanted to harness our powers, to use us for their own ends. I met others in captivity—Elementals, fae, and even a few creatures from the depths of the earth. We were all trapped, cut off from the forces that gave us life. The Institute saw us as resources, tools they could exploit.

'But they didn't understand that we weren't just magic to be tapped into. We were living, breathing parts of the natural world, and they were playing with forces they couldn't control. The balance of nature isn't something you can manipulate without consequences. I knew if they succeeded in their plans, they would disrupt the entire fabric of reality. The natural world and every creature connected to it would suffer.

'I never stopped thinking about the river, even when locked away. It called to me like a distant song just out of reach. It was a part of me, and I was a part of it. The Institute couldn't break that bond, no matter how hard they tried. Then, one day, my chance came.

'There was a disturbance in the facility—an explosion, maybe, or some magical surge. I don't know what caused it, but the containment field around my cell flickered briefly. It was enough. I felt a rush of power as I reconnected with the water in the pipes, the air, and the tiniest droplets that had seeped into the walls. I used every ounce of strength I had to break free, flooding the room and escaping into the facility.

'It wasn't easy. The Institute's agents were everywhere, and their machines were still trying to suppress my powers. But I had the water with me now, which strengthened me. I fought my way out, using the water to disable their machines, to blind them with mist and fog. I didn't stop until I reached the open air, where I felt the cool wind on my skin and inhaled the fresh scent of the river in the distance.

'That's when I saw Seraphina and Gisela, and they brought me here.' A dark shadow crossed her face. 'I miss my home. I miss the feel of the Tees flowing through my fingers, the sound of the current lulling me to sleep at night. But I can't go back—not yet. The Institute has taken too much from me, and I won't let them take anything else. I'm Peg Powler, a guardian of the river, and I'll do whatever it takes to protect the natural world from those who would harm it. The balance must be restored. And if that means taking down the Institute, so be it. They've made an enemy of the water, and they'll learn soon enough that you can't control what flows freely.'

Ella's parents listened with rapt attention, their scientific minds struggling to reconcile these fantastic descriptions with their understanding of reality. Andrew leaned forward, his brow furrowed in concentration. 'But how does it all work? What laws of physics govern the Elemental realm?'

Peg smiled, her form shimmering like sunlight on water. 'The laws of your science don't apply in the same way, Dr Finn. In the Elemental world, belief and imagination have as much power as gravity. The impossible becomes possible if you will it strongly enough.'

Gemma shook her head in amazement. 'It sounds beautiful. But also dangerous.'

'It is both,' Callisto rumbled. 'And that is why we must be vigilant. The balance between our worlds has always been precarious. Now, it seems, that balance is more dangerous than ever.'

All eyes turned to Seraphina. The witch had been

listening silently, her face pale in the firelight. Now, she straightened up, her eyes focusing on the group.

'What I'm about to tell you,' she began, her voice low and intense, 'is a legend passed down through generations of witches and warlocks. It's a story of darkness, of creatures so terrible that their existence threatens the fabric of reality.'

The hair on Ella's hands prickled as she leaned closer to her mother.

Chapter 4

The Soulless

Seraphina's words made the night around them grow darker, the shadows deeper.

'They are called The Soulless - winged creatures with claws on their hands and feet and faces like demonic bulls. They are not of Earth nor the Elemental realm. They come from elsewhere. A dimension of pure chaos and malevolence.'

Barbara's hand tightened on the hilt of her sword, her warrior's instincts responding to the threat in Seraphina's words. Kitty's fur stood on end, crackling with nervous energy. Veronica held her breath.

Seraphina continued. 'Hundreds of thousands of years ago, The Soulless opened a portal to Earth. They poured through in waves, wreaking havoc and destruction wherever they went. They saw humans as little more than cattle, to be dominated and ruled over.'

Seraphina's eyes grew distant as if she were seeing the ancient battle play out before her. 'The devastation was... unimaginable. Entire civilisations were wiped out. The land was scorched and twisted by their presence. It appeared all hope was lost.'

'But humanity didn't face this threat alone,' she added. 'The Elementals, sensing the danger to the delicate balance between worlds, joined the fight. It was a battle that raged across continents and dimensions, a war that reshaped the planet.'

Ella's mind raced, trying to comprehend the scale of what Seraphina was describing. Could history have forgotten such a cataclysmic event?

'In the end, The Soulless were driven back through great sacrifice and potent magic. The portal was sealed, and they were banished to their hellish dimension. But the cost was enormous. Many of the most powerful Elementals vanished in the final battle, and the human world was left in ruins, forced to rebuild from almost nothing.'

Seraphina stared at Ella. 'The Book of All Life, Ella, was created after this war. It's a repository of knowledge and power, a safeguard against the return of The Soulless. And now, it seems, that safeguard is needed once more.'

A heavy silence fell over the group as they absorbed her words. The fire crackled in the stillness.

Then, Andrew spoke, his voice strained. 'Are you saying these creatures are trying to return? That they're going to invade our world again?'

Seraphina nodded. 'The signs are there for those who know how to read them. The thinning of the veil between worlds and the increase in Elemental activity all point to a weakening of the ancient barriers.'

'But why now?' Gemma asked. 'Why after all this time?'

'Time flows differently in other dimensions,' Peg Powler

explained. 'What has been thousands of years for us may have been only moments for The Soulless. Or perhaps they have spent all this time searching for a way to break through.'

Delf's face was grim. 'Whatever the reason, if they return, the consequences will be catastrophic for the human world and the Elemental realm. The Soulless care nothing for the delicate balance between our worlds. They would consume everything in their path.'

'What can we do?' Ella asked. 'How do we stop them?'

Seraphina's gaze softened as she looked at Ella. 'That, my dear, is where you come in. The Book of All Life chose you for a reason. You have a connection to both worlds, human and Elemental. You may be the key to preventing this catastrophe.'

'But I don't know how,' Ella protested. 'I don't understand my abilities. How am I supposed to stop an invasion of demonic creatures?'

Agrius stepped forward, placing a comforting hand on Ella's shoulder. 'No hero starts their journey fully prepared, Ella. You have grown so much already, and you have all of us to support you.'

Callisto nodded her massive head in agreement. 'We will teach you what we know of our world and its magic. Together, we may strengthen the barriers and keep The Soulless at bay.'

'And don't forget,' Kitty added with a wink, 'you've got nine lives worth of luck on your side with me around.'

Despite the gravity of the situation, Ella smiled at the cat's quip. Looking at the circle of faces – human, Elemental, and everything in between – she felt a surge of hope. They were an unlikely group, thrown together by circumstance and danger, but there was strength in their diversity.

'Okay,' she said, squaring her shoulders. 'How do we begin?'

Seraphina smiled, a hint of her old resilience returning to her face. 'We start with the Book, Ella. It's time for you to begin your training. The fate of two worlds may depend on it.'

As the fire burned low and the stars wheeled overhead, the unlikely band of heroes began to plan. They had much to learn and little time to prepare, but they had something The Soulless could never understand – the power of friendship, of unity in the face of overwhelming odds.

Ella peered into the night sky, wondering what challenges lay ahead. Whatever came, she knew she wouldn't face it alone. With her friends and family by her side and the power of the Light within her, she was ready to take the next step on her extraordinary journey.

The island around them seemed to pulse with anticipation as if the land recognised the momentous task before them. In the distance, a bird called, its haunting cry a reminder of the wild magic that permeated this place. While the others spoke amongst themselves, Ella grabbed Seraphina's arm and pulled her to the side.

'Are you okay, child?' the witch asked.

Ella lowered her voice so only they could hear. 'Tonight, you said the Book of All Life was created after this war with The Soulless, right?'

Seraphina smiled. 'I'm glad you were paying attention.'

'Oh, I was doing more than that. Do you remember when we first met?'

'Of course, in that hospital where you begged me to save your horrible cousin.'

Ella grimaced. 'I don't know about that.'

'Your cousin hated you. All three of them did – Daisy, Dotty and Dolly.'

Ella didn't want to think about what had happened to her cousins. 'I didn't beg you to bring Dotty out of her coma.'

Seraphina shook her head. 'No? I must be remembering it differently.'

Ella frowned. 'Anyway, that's not what I meant. Pandora claimed she created the Book of All Life as a doorway between Earth and the Elemental realm after humans had banished the Elementals there.'

'This is true,' the witch said.

Frustration grew inside Ella. 'What? That she said it or that she did it?'

'Both. Pan created all life, remember?'

'I recall her claiming that,' Ella replied.

Seraphina shrugged. 'It makes no difference. Pandora was all-powerful on Earth until humans tricked her and the other Elementals, who they banished to another realm. Then, after thousands of years of exile, Pan was working her way back to what she thought was rightfully hers until you stopped her.'

Ella puffed out her cheeks. 'She would have destroyed everything. And you were helping her.'

'I made a mistake,' Seraphina said. 'Haven't I made up for it since?'

'I suppose so,' Ella replied.

The witch glanced at Gemma and Andrew Finn. 'Have you told them of the blood lineage that flows through Pandora into your mother and you?'

Ella's expression darkened. 'Not yet.'

'But you will?'

'When I get the chance but stop changing the subject. If

Pandora created the Book of All Life as a gateway for her and all the other banished Elementals to return to Earth, how was it created after this war with The Soulless?'

'Why didn't you ask this earlier?' Seraphina said.

'I was confused,' Ella answered.

Seraphina grinned. 'Of course. The war against The Soulless was long before humans banished Elementals from this planet. Humans and Elementals mostly lived in peace and harmony then. It was only later that things turned sour when *man* thought *he* was superior to everything and that all female power had to be eradicated from the planet. That's when Pandora finished the Book of All Life, but she started its creation after the defeat of The Soulless in case they returned. Little did she know her creations would turn against her.'

Ella considered this, unsure if the witch was telling the truth. Like Veronica Venus, she was uncertain if she could trust Seraphina. Yet both women had saved Ella and her parents.

'Was it The Soulless speaking through you?' Ella asked.

Seraphina shrugged. 'I'm not sure. I felt it inside my head wriggling like a worm.' She shuddered. 'It was something I've never encountered before.'

Ella glanced into the jungle. 'Why now?'

'This island is special. Perhaps the connection to the realm of The Soulless is at its strongest here. Or...?'

'Or what?'

'Or,' Seraphina replied. 'They know Pandora is no threat to them anymore.' She gazed at Ella. 'Isn't that right?'

Ella rolled her eyes. 'The last time I saw Dora, she was with a talking pink elephant.'

Seraphina grinned. 'Dora? She'd reverted to the child who pretended to be your friend?'

Ella nodded. 'Yeah, I think so, after I took all of her Light.'

'That's interesting,' Seraphina added. 'Wherever she is, Pandora or Dora, she's too weak to help us against The Soulless.'

Ella frowned. 'I don't want her help. We don't need her help. She was going to wipe out humanity, remember?'

'Indeed, but don't forget I'm not your enemy, Ella Finn.'

'Okay,' Ella said.

'You're welcome,' Seraphina replied. 'Now, if you don't mind, I must feed Gisela. She gets cranky if she goes hungry for too long.'

Ella watched her go, wondering what you feed a dragon, when she felt a tug on her sleeve. She turned to see Kitty Stardust, the talking cat's eyes glowing in the dying firelight.

'Come with me, dear,' Kitty whispered. 'There's something I think you should see.'

Curious, Ella followed Kitty to the edge of the clearing. The cat led her to a small, secluded meadow that Ella hadn't noticed before. In the centre stood a circle of standing stones, each etched with strange, glowing symbols.

'What is this place?' Ella asked in wonder, her fingers tracing the icy, rough surface of the nearest stone.

Kitty's tail swished. 'It's a nexus point where the energies of different realms converge. Seraphina created it when we first arrived on the island. It's helping to keep us hidden from the humans. Here, we can best sense the shifts and changes in the magical world, the flow of the Light.'

As if in response to Kitty's words, the symbols on the stones pulsed with a soft, blue illumination. Ella felt a tingling sensation in her fingertips, like static electricity but warmer, more alive.

'Close your eyes,' Kitty commanded. 'Reach out with

your senses, not just the physical ones, but with your inner Light. What do you feel?'

Ella did as instructed, closing her eyes and trying to quiet her racing thoughts. At first, she felt nothing but the night air on her skin and heard only the gentle rustling of leaves. Then, gradually, she noticed something else. It was like an immense, invisible web stretching out in all directions. She sensed the pulse of life in the forest around her, the slow, ancient thoughts of the trees, the quick, darting consciousness of small animals.

And beyond that, she detected a presence - a vast, roiling darkness pressed against the edges of her perception. It was hungry, malevolent, held at bay by only the thinnest of barriers. It felt alien, waiting for her in the vastness of space. Whispering to her.

Come to me.

Ella's eyes snapped open, her heart racing. 'I felt it,' she gasped. 'The darkness. The Soulless. They're out there, aren't they?'

Kitty nodded. 'Yes, they are. But don't be afraid, Ella. What you just did, sensing the energies around you, that's the first step in learning to control and direct them. You can strengthen those barriers to push against the void with practice.'

As they returned to the camp, Ella's mind buzzed with questions and possibilities. But instead of feeling overwhelmed, she felt a growing sense of determination. She'd been given an incredible gift, a chance to make a real difference in the world – in multiple worlds.

Back in her tent, Ella grabbed the Book of All Life. Its cover seemed to warm at her touch, the paper rustling as if stirred by an unfelt breeze. As she opened it, the symbols on the pages – the images of Elementals – shifted and changed.

'Are you okay?' her mother said behind her.

Ella put the book down and turned. 'Just tired, that's all.'

Gemma Finn sat opposite her daughter. 'Have you told us everything you know about that book?'

Ella nodded. 'Yes, Mum, all of it – Elementals, the multiverse, the Light. Everything.'

But not Pandora and how they were related to the so-called Creator. And not how Ella had wiped their memories.'

Her mother patted her hand. 'Okay, love. You get some sleep. Seraphina says we all have a big day ahead of us tomorrow.'

Ella watched her mother leave, ignoring the whispering in her head.

Chapter 5

Eight Miles High

The morning sun had crested the horizon when Seraphina shook Ella awake. 'Rise and shine, young one,' the witch whispered, her eyes twinkling with excitement. 'We have quite the adventure ahead of us.'

Ella rubbed the sleep from her face, her mind sharpening as she remembered the previous night's events. 'What's happening?'

Seraphina smiled. 'We're taking a little trip. You, me, and your mother. It's time you saw this island from a different perspective.'

Intrigued, Ella dressed and emerged from her tent to find her mother awake, looking nervous and excited. Gemma Finn gave her daughter a quick hug. 'Seraphina says we're going flying.'

Before Ella could respond, a massive shadow passed overhead. She watched Gisela circling the camp. The dragon's scales shimmered in the light, shifting colours like an oil slick on water.

Seraphina clapped her hands together. 'Well then, shall we be off?'

Ella marvelled at the dragon's size as they neared where Gisela had landed. She was as large as a bus, with wings that seemed to span half the clearing when extended. Gisela's eyes, each the size of dinner plates, regarded them with a thrilling and unnerving intelligence. Seraphina approached the dragon, speaking in a language that sounded like whispers and musical notes. Gisela responded with a low rumble Ella felt in her bones.

'She says she's delighted to give us a tour of the island,' Seraphina translated, turning back to Ella and Gemma. 'Shall we?'

With surprising grace for such a large creature, Gisela lowered her head and extended one of her wings like a ramp. Seraphina climbed up first, showing them where to sit among the dragon's neck ridges. As Ella settled into place behind Seraphina, with her mother behind her, she felt excitement and trepidation. She'd experienced many magical things, but flying on a dragon was fantastic, an experience she'd already had when Seraphina and the dragon had brought them to the island.

'Hold on tight,' Seraphina called over her shoulder. 'And whatever you do, don't look down... at least not right away!'

With a mighty leap, Gisela launched herself into the air. Ella's stomach lurched as they climbed, the ground falling away. She heard her mother gasp behind her, fingers digging into Ella's sides.

Ella dared to look down as they levelled out, soaring above the treetops. The sight left her speechless. The island stretched beneath them, a tapestry of greens and blues. Half of the landmass was covered in dense jungle, a riot of emerald hues that seemed to pulse with life even from such a height.

'It's incredible,' Ella breathed, her eyes wide as she tried to take in every detail.

'Indeed it is,' Seraphina agreed. 'This island is unlike any other place on Earth. It exists in a sort of in-between space, not fully in your world or ours. That's what makes it the perfect sanctuary.'

Gemma spoke as Gisela banked to the right, giving them a panoramic view of the coastline. 'The shape of the island... the location...' She paused, her scientific mind working overtime. 'Seraphina, could this be part of Doggerland?'

Seraphina turned, an impressed look on her face. 'Very astute, Dr Finn. Yes, this is part of what your archaeologists call Doggerland - a piece preserved and hidden by powerful magic when the rest sank beneath the waves thousands of years ago.'

Ella, who had learned about Doggerland in school, felt excited. 'So we're flying over a prehistoric landscape?'

'In a manner of speaking, yes,' Seraphina nodded. 'Though it's been changed and shaped by magical forces over the millennia. Keep your eyes open - you're about to see things no modern human has ever witnessed.'

As if on cue, Gisela dipped lower, skimming over the jungle treetops. Ella gasped as she spotted movement below - creatures resembling a cross between monkeys and birds, swinging from branch to branch with multi-coloured wings.

'Avians,' Seraphina explained. 'Elemental beings that evolved to inhabit the space between earth and sky.'

They flew on, passing over a vast meadow where flowers the size of houses bloomed in impossible colours.

Ella saw herds of animals grazing among the gigantic petals, but she couldn't make out the details.

As they neared the island's centre, Ella noticed a glint of something that didn't seem to belong in the primaeval landscape. 'What's that?' she called out, pointing.

Gisela banked again, circling lower. As they approached, Ella's jaw dropped. Rising from the jungle canopy was a pyramid, its smooth sides gleaming gold in the morning sun.

'That,' Seraphina said, her voice filled with awe, 'is something I've never seen before. That pyramid has never revealed itself in all my time studying this island.'

Gemma leaned forward, her scientific curiosity overriding any lingering fear of their precarious position. 'It looks almost Egyptian in design, but the material... it's not like any stone I've ever seen.'

As they circled the pyramid, Ella noticed strange symbols etched into its surface, glowing with a faint blue light similar to the standing stones in the meadow. 'Those markings,' she said, 'they look like the ones on the Book of All Life's cover, but I don't recognise the Elementals.'

Seraphina nodded, her expression thoughtful. 'Yes, indeed. I've met many more Elementals than you, Ella, but I don't recognise those figures. This is a powerful place steeped in ancient magic. We'll need to investigate it further, but not today. For now, let's finish our tour.'

Gisela carried them onward, over more wonders that defied description - a lake whose waters flowed uphill in a perpetual waterfall, a grove of trees with crystal leaves that chimed in the wind, a valley where the rocks seemed to shift and move like living creatures.

As they circled back towards their camp, Ella's mind reeled with all she'd seen. The island was far more vast and magical than she had ever imagined, and the mysterious pyramid at its heart raised more questions than answers.

Gisela landed with surprising gentleness in the clearing. As they dismounted, Ella's legs wobbled, a combination of the long flight and the overwhelming experience.

'That was...' Gemma began, shaking her head in amazement. 'I don't even have words for what that was.'

Seraphina smiled. 'It's a lot to take in, I know. However, comprehending the full scope of this place is crucial to understanding what lies ahead. Come, let's gather the others. We have much to discuss.'

As they returned to the camp, Ella's mind whirred with questions. What was the pyramid? How was it connected to the Book of All Life? And most importantly, could it hold the key to stopping The Soulless?

The rest of the group awaited their return, gathered around the remnants of the previous night's fire. Veronica, Catherine, Agrius, Callisto, Kitty Stardust, Delf, Peg Powler, Barbara, and Ella's father looked up as they approached.

'Well?' Andrew asked, standing to embrace his wife and daughter. 'How was it?'

Ella, Gemma, and Seraphina took turns describing what they'd seen for the next hour. The others listened with rapt attention, sometimes interjecting with questions or expressions of awe.

When they reached the part about the pyramid, a hush fell over the group. Delf the Elf's eyes widened in recognition. 'A golden pyramid with glowing symbols? I've heard legends of such a structure, but I always thought they were just stories.'

'What legends?' Ella asked.

Delf's brow furrowed in concentration. 'In the

Elemental world, there are tales of ancient nexus points - places where the barriers between dimensions are at their thinnest. These nexus points were marked by great structures, built by beings of immense power to stabilise and control the energy flow between worlds.'

Seraphina nodded. 'That aligns with some of the lore I've studied. If this pyramid is such a nexus point, it could explain why this part of Doggerland was preserved when the rest sank.'

'At the Institute,' Veronica said. 'Our scientists were studying the portals we discovered in Britain, but they always appeared as shimmering multi-coloured circles of various sizes. They weren't buildings or structures.'

Ella glanced at mother and daughter, seeing the confusion in Catherine Venus's eyes and wondered how much Veronica had told her about this dangerous new reality.

'There was a house on Saltburn cliffs that only I could see,' Ella said. 'That was like a halfway house between Earth and the Elemental world.'

'But what does it mean for us now?' Barbara asked, her warrior's mind already strategising. 'Could this nexus point be connected to the threat of The Soulless?'

A thoughtful silence fell over the group. It was Kitty Stardust who spoke. 'If the pyramid is a nexus point, it could be both a danger and an opportunity. On the one hand, it could be a weak point that The Soulless might exploit to break through to our world.'

'On the other hand,' Peg Powler continued, catching Kitty's train of thought, 'if we could learn to control it, we might be able to use it to strengthen the barriers between dimensions.'

Ella's heart raced with the implications. 'So the pyramid could be the key to stopping The Soulless invasion?'

Seraphina touched Ella's shoulder. 'It's possible. But we shouldn't get ahead of ourselves. This is ancient, powerful magic we're dealing with. We'll need to approach it carefully.'

Andrew spoke. 'I may not understand all this talk of magic and dimensions, but I know about research and investigation. We must study this pyramid to gather as much information as possible before considering using it.'

Gemma nodded in agreement. 'Andrew's right. We should organise an expedition to the pyramid. We'll document the symbols, take measurements, and maybe even collect samples if they're safe.'

'I'll help translate the symbols,' Delf offered. 'Between my knowledge of ancient Elemental languages and the Book of All Life, we might be able to decipher their meaning.'

Callisto rumbled her agreement. 'And I can provide protection. If this place is as powerful as we suspect, it may have its own defences.'

As the group continued to plan, Ella felt excitement and apprehension. The pyramid represented hope - a potential way to stop The Soulless and protect the human and Elemental worlds. But it was also a leap into the unknown, fraught with possible dangers.

She thought of the Book of All Life, hidden in her tent. The strange symbols on the pyramid looked similar to those in the Book. Was this the next step in her journey to understand her powers and place in the coming conflict?

As if reading her thoughts, Seraphina caught Ella's eye. 'Remember, Ella, you are at the centre of this. The Book chose you for a reason. Whatever we discover at the pyramid, you will play a crucial role in unravelling its mysteries.'

Ella nodded, feeling the weight of responsibility settle

on her. But as she studied the diverse group of beings surrounding her, she felt a surge of confidence. Whatever challenges lay ahead, she wouldn't face them alone.

The unlikely band continued their planning as the sun climbed higher in the sky, casting dappled shadows through the canopy above. The mysterious pyramid at the island's heart beckoned promising answers but also untold dangers.

Ella's mind wandered back to the aerial view of the island. From above, it had seemed like a hidden paradise, a sanctuary from the troubles of the outside world. Now she understood it was much more than that. The island, with its strange creatures, powerful magic, and ancient secrets, might be the key to saving her world and the Elemental realm from the encroaching darkness of The Soulless.

As the others discussed logistics and safety precautions for their expedition, Ella slipped away, returning to her tent. She retrieved the Book of All Life, its cover warm to her touch. Finding a quiet spot at the edge of the clearing, she opened the book, its pages seeming to glow in the dappled sunlight. She was so engrossed she didn't notice Agrius approaching until his shadow fell across the paper.

'Studying hard, I see,' the centaur said, his voice gentle.

She looked up, blinking as her eyes adjusted. 'I want to be prepared. There's so much I still don't understand.'

He nodded, lowering himself to sit beside her. 'Knowledge is indeed power, Ella. But remember, true wisdom comes from more than just books; it comes from experience and the counsel of friends. Each being here has unique insights and abilities. The strength of this group lies not just in our individual powers but in how we work together.'

She considered his words, realising the truth in them. 'You're right,' she said, closing the book. 'I shouldn't isolate myself. We're in this together.'

As they rejoined the others, Ella felt a renewed sense of purpose. The pyramid and its secrets awaited them, holding the potential to change everything. But whatever they discovered there, Ella knew the real power lay in the bonds between her friends and allies.

'We'll visit the pyramid tomorrow,' Seraphina said. 'All of us, since I don't think we should separate from now.'

Ella studied the witch's face. 'Are you okay?'

Seraphina gave a weary smile. 'Keeping the island hidden from human eyes is using all my powers. There seems to be increased activity in the air above us.'

'Planes?' Andrew asked.

The witch nodded. 'Several a day.'

'The Institute?' Veronica said.

'Probably,' Seraphina replied. 'Though they won't be the only ones. It's not just the British interested in Elementals – most other major nations have similar organisations who will know what happened in Teesside.'

'We have little time then,' Veronica added. 'We have to get some answers from this pyramid tomorrow.'

The group retired for the night, expectation and anxiety rising in all of them.

Chapter 6

We Are Family

They woke to bad news.

'I can't go with you,' Veronica Venus said. 'Cat is ill.'

Gemma Finn went to comfort Veronica. Ella studied Venus's face, still amazed Venus had worked for the Institute a short while ago. That secret government organisation collected Elementals for study and had discovered several dimensional portals in Britain. Those two things had led them to Ella in the north of England. And Venus had tricked Ella, putting Ella's parents in danger, to use Ella and the Book of All Life for the Institute's nefarious reasons.

Ella grimaced, remembering how the Institute had poisoned her mother and father as leverage against her. In their studies – and experiments – the Institute had discovered that physical contact between Elementals and humans could cure sickness and ill health. Ella knew it was because of the Light inside Elementals. That's why the Institute, led by Director Gideon Black, had poisoned Andrew and Gemma Finn, threatened Ella and her friends Hannah and Billy, and blackmailed Ella into handing over the Book of All Life and revealing its secrets.

They would have succeeded, and Ella would have lost everything if it hadn't been for Venus. Seeing Black's treatment of the Finns and discovering how the Institute was hurting Elementals convinced Veronica to betray her employers and help Ella. But Ella still didn't know if she trusted her.

'What's wrong with Catherine?' Ella asked.

Veronica turned to them all. 'Two years ago, my daughter Catherine – Cat – was studying in Newcastle when creatures attacked people near the quayside.'

'Creatures?' Gemma Finn said.

'Harpies,' Veronica answered. 'That's what invaded Newcastle that day. Nobody knew what they were then, but the Institute found out later - half-human, half-bird creatures with pale, haggard faces and massive claws on their hands and feet. Several people died, but Cat survived, stuck in a coma. In my work with the Institute, we discovered that contact between Elementals and humans could cure illnesses we believed were incurable. Once I realised this, there was only one thing on my mind – to use an Elemental to revive Cat from her coma. That's why I followed Director Black's orders, even though I knew they were illegal and unethical.' Veronica looked at Ella. 'That's why I worked against you and your parents until I came to my senses.' She touched Ella's shoulder. 'And that's why I'll always be grateful to you and Seraphina for rescuing Cat from the coma and bringing her back to me.'

Veronica nodded at the witch, and Seraphina returned the gesture.

'But Cat's still not well?' Ella said.

Veronica confirmed that. 'She's getting there, but this is

all very emotional for her. We've not had a proper talk since Seraphina took her from the hospital in Newcastle and brought us all to this island.' She smiled at everyone. 'I was in the army the last time we talked, before the incident in Newcastle. I haven't explained to her about why I left the military and joined the Institute, and there's the fact that...'

She trailed off, unable to finish her train of thought.

'Cat still remembers what happened with the harpies,' Ella said.

Veronica nodded. 'She has a scar on the back of her head, which is a constant reminder.' Her lips trembled. 'And then this morning, I woke to find her shivering in the corner, even though it's hot here. She can't leave the tent. Physically, she appears fine, but emotionally, there's a long way to go.'

Ella's heart went out to them. While she still harboured some mistrust towards Veronica because of their complicated history, Ella couldn't help but empathise with the pain and worry on the woman's face.

'I'll stay with you and Cat,' Gemma offered, placing a comforting hand on Veronica's arm. 'The others can explore and search for the pyramid.'

Veronica shook her head. 'No, you should all go. Cat and I will be fine here in the camp. Maybe some quiet time together is what we need.'

After some discussion, it was agreed. Ella, Gemma, Seraphina, and the rest would venture into the dense jungle, searching for the ancient pyramid, while Veronica remained behind to care for her daughter. Agrius and Gisela would remain as protection.

As the exploration party prepared to depart, Ella glanced at the tent where Catherine rested. A pang of guilt twisted in her stomach - should she offer to stay and help?

No, Veronica had insisted they go on without her. Perhaps mother and daughter needed the time alone to reconnect and heal.

The group said their goodbyes and set off into the lush greenery with backpacks loaded and water bottles filled. Veronica ducked into the tent where Catherine lay curled on her sleeping bag. The girl's eyes were open, staring at the canvas wall.

She knelt beside her daughter. 'How are you feeling, sweetheart?'

Catherine didn't respond at first. Then, in a quiet voice: 'Cold. I'm so cold, Mum.'

Veronica's brow furrowed with concern. She pressed a hand to Catherine's forehead but felt no fever. Outside, the temperature was climbing as the tropical sun rose higher.

'You're not feverish,' Veronica murmured. 'Here, let me get you another blanket.'

Her mind raced as she wrapped a light cover around Catherine's shoulders. Was this some lingering effect from the harpy attack? A psychological response to the trauma? Or something else?

She smoothed Catherine's hair back from her face. 'Do you want to talk about it?'

Catherine's eyes squeezed shut. 'I keep seeing them,' she whispered. 'Those things, with their horrible faces and claws. I hear them screaming.'

Veronica's heart clenched. 'Oh, Cat. I'm so sorry. You're safe now. Those creatures can't hurt you anymore.'

'But they're out there somewhere, aren't they?' Catherine's voice trembled. 'In some other world. What if they come back?'

Veronica hesitated, unsure how to respond. She hadn't

yet explained everything about Elementals and dimensional portals to Catherine. How much should she reveal?

'The people we're travelling with - Ella, Seraphina, and the others - are working to ensure nothing like that happens again. You don't need to worry.'

Catherine's eyes opened, focusing on her mother. 'But you're afraid. I can see it.'

Veronica sighed. Her daughter had always been perceptive. 'I suppose I am, but not of those creatures. I'm afraid of losing you again. Of failing you.'

Tears welled in Catherine's eyes. 'You didn't fail me, Mum. You saved me.'

'Oh, Cat.' Veronica gathered her daughter into her arms, holding her close as Catherine's tears soaked into her shirt. Her own eyes stung as she stroked Catherine's hair. 'I love you so much. We'll get through this together, I promise.'

As mother and daughter clung to each other, the sounds of the jungle faded away. For a moment, it was just the two of them, finding comfort and strength in each other's embrace. Veronica sat cross-legged beside Catherine's sleeping form. The girl had drifted off after their tearful heart-to-heart, exhausted.

She watched the gentle rise and fall of her daughter's chest, marvelling at how young and vulnerable Catherine looked in sleep. She couldn't believe she was nearly twenty - in Veronica's mind, she was still that bright-eyed little girl with scraped knees and an insatiable curiosity about everything.

So much had changed since then - Veronica's military career, her work with the Institute, and the harpy attack that could have taken Catherine from her forever. It all felt like a lifetime ago.

Now, they were on a remote jungle island with a group of virtual strangers, caught up in a world of Elementals and interdimensional intrigue. Veronica still struggled to comprehend it. She sighed, rubbing her temples. How could she explain all of this to Catherine? How could she make her daughter understand her choices and the lines she'd crossed in her desperation to save her?

A warm breeze rustled the tent flap, carrying with it the verdant scents of the jungle. Veronica inhaled them all. One step at a time, she reminded herself. Catherine was alive, awake, and healing. That was what mattered most. The rest, well, they would figure it out together.

She busied herself with minor tasks around the camp as the day wore on. She organised their supplies, filled water containers, and attempted to rig a simple lean-to for extra shade.

All the while, she kept a watchful eye on Catherine. The girl stirred, muttering in her sleep, but didn't wake.

It was late afternoon when she opened her eyes, blinking in the golden light filtering through the tent walls. 'Mum?'

Veronica was at her side in an instant. 'I'm here, sweetheart. How are you feeling?'

Catherine considered for a moment. 'Better, I think. Not so cold anymore.'

Relief washed over Veronica. 'That's good. Are you hungry? I can heat some soup.'

Catherine nodded, sitting up. As Veronica busied herself with their small camping stove, she watched her daughter study their surroundings with wide eyes.

'Where exactly are we? I remember bits and pieces. Flying. But everything's hazy.'

Veronica hesitated, stirring the broth. How much should she reveal? 'We're on an island. It's a long story.'

Catherine's brow furrowed. 'Does it have something to do with those creatures that attacked me?'

Veronica took a deep breath, steeling herself. 'Yes, in a way. But it's complicated.'

'Then un-complicate it,' Catherine said, a hint of her old fire creeping into her voice. 'Please, Mum. I'm tired of feeling lost and confused. I want to understand what's happening.'

She met her daughter's gaze, seeing the determination there. 'All right. I'll try to explain. But I need you to keep an open mind. Some of what I'm about to tell you may sound impossible.'

As the soup simmered, Veronica talked. She told Catherine about Elementals, dimensional portals, the Institute and its nefarious goals. She explained about Ella and the others and how she'd escaped from the Institute to this hidden island.

Catherine listened in stunned silence, her food forgotten. When her mother stopped, the only sound was the gentle bubbling of the pot and the distant calls of jungle birds.

'So, you're saying magic is real?' Catherine said. 'That there are other worlds out there, full of incredible creatures and powers?'

Veronica nodded. 'I know it sounds ridiculous. I didn't believe it myself at first. But I've seen things, Cat. Things that defy all rational explanations. And I'm not sure if it's magic as we think of it. It's more to do with the Light inside us, especially in Elementals.'

Catherine was quiet for a long moment, processing.

Then, to Veronica's surprise, a small smile tugged at her lips.

'You know,' Catherine said, 'when I was little, I always daydreamed about magic being real. About having secret powers or going on grand adventures.' Her grin faded. 'I guess I got my wish, in a way. Though not quite how I imagined it.'

Veronica squeezed her daughter's hand. 'I'm sorry you were pulled into all this, Cat. If I could go back and change things...'

Catherine shook her head. 'You can't, Mum. What's done is done.' She took a deep breath, squaring her shoulders. 'So what happens now?'

Veronica blinked, taken aback by the sudden determination in her daughter's voice. 'What do you mean?'

'What's our next move?' Catherine's eyes were bright with a familiar spark - the same fierce curiosity that had driven her since childhood. 'Ella and the others are searching for some ancient pyramid, right? There must be something we can do to help.'

Veronica stared at her daughter in amazement. After everything Catherine had been through, after the fear and trauma she'd experienced just that morning, she was ready to dive headfirst into this strange new world.

A swell of pride and love rose in Veronica's chest. Her little girl had grown into a remarkable young woman, stronger and braver than she had ever given her credit for.

'Well,' Veronica said, a slow smile spreading across her face, 'I'll tell you what I discovered while working for the Institute. How does that sound?'

Catherine Venus smiled at her mother. 'Like I'm alive again.'

Chapter 7

The Heart of Darkness

Barbara led the way, scanning for danger. Callisto followed, her massive form pushing through the dense undergrowth. Kitty Stardust trailed her, her multi-coloured fur shimmering in the dappled sunlight. Delf moved with ethereal grace while Peg Powler seemed to flow like water over the uneven terrain. Gemma and Andrew Finn followed them, their scientific curiosity palpable even in the face of the unknown. Seraphina and Ella brought up the rear. Ella had thought her parents would have wanted her to stay behind, surprised they'd come to terms with her connection to a strange and wonderful new existence.

Well, it was wonderful as long as it wasn't trying to kidnap or kill her.

'Don't we need a map?' she said.

Seraphina tapped her nose. 'After our trip in the sky yesterday, I know where it is. It just won't be easy getting there.'

The sounds of the jungle enveloped them – a cacophony of bird calls, insect buzzes, and the distant screech of creatures Ella couldn't name. The air was rich with the scent of damp earth, exotic flowers, and something else - a faint metallic trace that seemed to grow stronger as they moved deeper into the forest.

As they picked their way along barely visible trails, sweat beaded on Ella's forehead and trickled down her back. The humidity was suffocating, clinging to her like a second skin. She was grateful for the shade provided by the towering trees, their leafy boughs stretching far above. The going was slow and difficult. Thick vines and gnarled roots sought to trip them at every step. Thorny plants snagged at their clothing. The air grew more stifling as they moved further from the coast, heavy with moisture and the potent scent of flowers.

Ella's shirt clung to her back. She took a swig from her water bottle, grimacing at the tepid liquid. Even in the canopy's shade, the heat was intense.

She wiped the sweat from her brow. 'How much further do you think?'

Seraphina shrugged. 'Hard to say for certain. These jungles can be deceptive. But I'd estimate we're about halfway there.'

Gemma groaned. 'Only halfway? I feel like we've been walking for hours.'

'We have,' the witch said with a wry smile. 'Ancient ruins don't tend to be conveniently located, I'm afraid.'

As they rested, Ella's thoughts drifted back to Veronica and Catherine. She couldn't shake a nagging worry about leaving them behind.

'Do you think they'll be okay?' she asked. 'Veronica and Cat, I mean.'

Gemma's expression softened. 'I hope so, dear. Catherine's been through a terrible ordeal. But having her mother there will help, I'm sure.'

Seraphina nodded. 'Veronica may have made mistakes in the past, but her love for her daughter is genuine. Sometimes, that's the most powerful healing magic of all.'

Ella mulled this over as they resumed their trek. The relationship between Veronica and Catherine was so different from her own experience with her parents. Though she loved them dearly, their connection had felt distant recently, like an invisible barrier between them.

It may have been invisible, but Ella knew what it was – her guilt for not telling them everything. But how do you tell your mother she might be a descendant of a God-like creature who claimed to have created all life? After that revelation, perhaps she could explain how she'd wiped their memories of Pandora, portals, and strange realms.

Lost in those thoughts, she almost walked straight into a massive web between two trees. She yelped in surprise, stumbling backwards.

'Careful!' Seraphina steadied her. 'Best to watch where you're going.'

Ella shuddered, eyeing the web. Its silvery strands glistened with dew. A spider, the size of her palm, lurked at its centre, its legs banded in vivid orange and black.

'That's a golden orb weaver,' Seraphina explained. 'Impressive, isn't it? Their silk is incredibly strong - stronger than steel, in fact.'

'Fascinating,' Ella muttered, giving the web a wide berth as they continued. She made a mental note to be more alert to her surroundings.

A chorus of harsh screeches erupted from the trees to emphasise the point. Ella's heart leapt into her throat as she whirled, searching for the source of the commotion. A troop of monkeys came swinging through the branches; their long tails curled as they jumped from tree to tree. Their reddish-brown fur gleamed in patches of sunlight breaking through the canopy.

'Spider monkeys,' Gemma said with a delighted smile. 'Aren't they marvellous?'

Ella watched in awe as the acrobatic primates moved with fluid grace high above. Their cries faded as they swung deeper into the jungle.

'Do you smell that?' she asked, wrinkling her nose.

Kitty's whiskers twitched. 'Indeed. It's the aroma of old magic, dear. We're getting closer to the pyramid.'

As they pushed on, the vegetation grew denser, more alien. Vines with iridescent leaves twisted around trees with bark that pulsed with an inner light. Flowers the size of footballs opened and closed as they passed, releasing puffs of glittering pollen.

Andrew examined an extraordinary plant, its stem coiled like a spring and topped with what looked like tiny, spinning galaxies. 'Fascinating,' he murmured, reaching out to touch it.

'I wouldn't if I were you,' Delf warned, pulling him back. 'Some of these flora have unusual defences.'

To prove his point, a nearby shrub trembled, its leaves unfurling to reveal rows of gleaming teeth. They hurried past, Gemma muttering, 'Carnivorous plants are one thing, but that's just excessive.'

The ground sloped upward, and the trees thinned out. Barbara held up a hand, signalling the group to stop. 'Listen.'

For a moment, all Ella heard was the ambient noise of the jungle and her heartbeat. Then she caught it – a low, rhythmic drone that seemed to vibrate through her bones.

'It's coming from ahead,' Peg Powler said, her watery form rippling with excitement.

They pressed on, the humming growing louder with each step. The air shimmered like heat waves rising from a hot pavement but tinged with blues and purples. Ella's skin tingled, similar to what she'd experienced at the standing stones but far more intense.

They emerged from the treeline into a vast clearing. Ella's breath caught in her throat. Before them stood the golden pyramid, even more magnificent up close. Its smooth sides gleamed in the sunlight, the strange symbols etched into its surface pulsing with eerie blue light.

'By the Allfather,' Barbara breathed, her usual stoic demeanour cracking in awe.

Callisto rumbled, a sound of equal parts warning and wonder. 'There is great power here. We must tread carefully.'

As they approached the pyramid's base, Ella felt the Book of All Life in her backpack growing warmer as if responding to the energy emanating from the structure.

Delf stepped forward, his brow furrowed in concentration as he studied the glyphs. 'These are unlike any Elemental creatures I've ever seen. But there's something familiar about them.'

Kitty Stardust padded up next to him. 'You're right. It's as if they're speaking to me, but in a language I've forgotten.'

Gemma pulled out a camera, snapping photos. 'We'll need to document everything. There might be clues in the arrangement or repetition of these figures.'

As the others circled the pyramid, taking measurements and notes, Ella felt drawn to a particular section. The symbols seemed to glow brighter, pulsing with her heartbeat. Without thinking, she reached out to touch them.

'Ella, wait!' Andrew shouted, but it was too late.

When she touched the golden surface, energy surged through her. The world around her blurred and shifted, and for a moment, she saw not the jungle but a vast, star-filled void. Shapes moved in the darkness – massive, winged forms with glowing eyes and razor-sharp claws. The Soulless.

Just as quickly as it had come, the vision faded. She stumbled backwards, caught by Barbara's powerful arms before she could fall.

'What happened? What did you see?' the Valkyrie asked, her voice urgent.

Ella shook her head, trying to clear the images from her mind. 'I saw... I think I saw where The Soulless are from. And...' she swallowed hard, 'I think they saw me.'

A heavy silence fell over the group as they absorbed the implications of Ella's words. The jungle around them seemed darker, the air charged with an electric tension.

Peg Powler moved closer, her watery form rippling with concern. 'We've opened a door we might be unable to close.'

The humming from the pyramid intensified as if in response, the symbols glowing brighter. The ground trembled.

'Everyone, back to the treeline!' Barbara ordered, her warrior instincts taking over.

As they retreated to the relative safety of the jungle's edge, Ella sensed everything had changed. The pyramid was more than just an ancient structure or a nexus point. It was a beacon, a challenge - perhaps their only hope against the coming darkness.

'What should we do?' Ella asked.

'We find an entrance,' Seraphina said. 'Spread out and look, but touch nothing.'

They did as instructed, with Ella sticking close to Seraphina and thinking of the brief glimpse she got of The Soulless. She shivered as heat wrapped around her like a blanket. The scorching sun beat down mercilessly as the group studied the structure. The walls appeared to shimmer in the haze. Ella drank more from her water bottle, wondering if she should have stayed behind with Veronica and Cat. She trudged through the thick grass, swatting away buzzing insects and glancing at the witch, who seemed not bothered by the sun.

'Are we doing the right thing?' she asked.

Seraphina turned to Ella. 'What do you mean?'

Ella watched as her parents and the others continued walking around the pyramid. 'Perhaps we should have told somebody about this?'

'Who?' Seraphina said.

Ella shrugged. 'I don't know. The Institute, maybe.'

Seraphina looked surprised. 'You'd do that after all they did to you? After they poisoned your mother and father?'

Ella's shoulders slumped. 'No, of course not. I don't know what I was thinking.' She glanced at the pyramid. 'But if behind there are The Soulless, creatures it took the combined might of humans and Elementals to defeat – and Pandora – I wonder what we can do to stop them.'

Seraphina touched Ella's shoulder. 'They're not here.'

'I know, but what if it wasn't a warning that came through you but a trick to get us here and open this thing up, and they're just waiting inside to escape?'

The witch considered her words. 'You might be right. We can't stay on this island forever – it was only supposed to be a temporary resting place. We could leave here and forget about this pyramid.'

'Where would we go?' Ella asked.

'I've spoken to Veronica about this,' Seraphina replied. 'From her work at the Institute, she has contacts worldwide who might help us. And getting her daughter proper medical help is probably a good idea.'

Relief swept through Ella. 'I've been thinking about what to do when we leave here.'

'Yes?'

'The world needs to see the truth about Elementals,' Ella said. 'And what the Institute and similar organisations have done to harm them.'

Seraphina swatted away an annoying insect. 'And how would you do that?'

'It's simple. You, me and the others go on live TV and say what we know. The world will have to believe us then.'

'It's not that easy. Humans have encountered Elementals for centuries. Even after we were all banished from Earth to the other realm, there were still gaps between the worlds – portals – where Elementals would slip through from time to time. But they were always reported as fakes, lies, hallucinations or dreams. Even when you used the Book of All Life to bring Elementals to this world, people didn't believe what they witnessed with their own eyes, did they?'

'No, but it will be different this time. I'm sure of it.'

Seraphina shrugged. 'I guess we can only try.'

Ella beamed.

Then her mother shouted.

'The entrance is here!'

Chapter 8

Song to the Siren

As they neared the pyramid, Seraphina spoke. 'Be careful where you step.'

Andrew returned from his reconnaissance, frowning. 'The entrance looks clear, but there's something off about it. I can't quite put my finger on it.'

Delf raised an eyebrow. 'Off how? Magical off? Trap off? We're all going to die horribly off?'

'None of the above, I hope,' Andrew replied. 'Just... different from what I expected. You'll see when we get there.'

As they approached the entrance, Ella saw what her father meant. The blocks forming the doorway were too perfectly aligned, and the edges were too crisp for a structure of this age. It was as if someone had restored only this part of the pyramid, leaving the rest to the ravages of time.

Seraphina touched the surface. 'This stone's not limestone. It feels almost metallic.'

Gemma peered at the hieroglyphs carved into the entrance. 'These figures... some of them look familiar, but others...' She shook her head. 'I've not seen anything like them before.'

Andrew's eyes widened. 'Impossible. These glyphs are a mix of Ancient Egyptian and something I've only encountered in theoretical texts about...'

'About what?' Ella prompted.

Her father hesitated. 'About the possibility of extra-terrestrial influence on ancient cultures. But that's just fringe theory. It can't be...'

Kitty Stardust's tail twitched. 'Well, we won't find out standing out here in this heat. Shall we?'

They stepped into the gloom of the pyramid. As their eyes adjusted, they entered a long corridor, its walls covered in intricate carvings and paintings. The symbols etched into the stone flickered with an eerie, pulsing blue light as if the structure were alive, watching them.

Ella took a deep breath, the musty air from the entrance seeping into her lungs, carrying with it the weight of centuries. Behind her, the dense jungle, so full of life moments ago, seemed to fall away, swallowed by the oppressive energy emanating from the pyramid. The dampness clung to her skin, but the cool draft coming from inside was refreshing, like a breeze sweeping out of an ancient tomb.

'Let's have some illumination,' Seraphina said. She raised her hand, and a bright light sprang from her palm. 'I can't keep this up for long without weakening the barrier keeping the island invisible, so we'll have to make this quick.'

The walls came alive with colour - vibrant blues, reds, and golds that had no right to be so well-preserved after so much time.

'Look at this,' Gemma breathed, gesturing to a detailed scene. It depicted human-like figures standing alongside beings that defied description - some with animal heads, others with too many limbs, and ones seemingly made of pure light.

'Humans with Elementals?' Ella said.

'It's a history,' Barbara murmured, eyes scanning the hieroglyphs. 'But not like any I've seen before. It speaks of visitors from the stars, of knowledge given and technology shared.'

Callisto growled, her keen senses alert for any danger. Peg Powler, who had been quiet, spoke up. 'There's water nearby. I can feel it.'

Andrew nodded. 'Many pyramids had symbolic rivers running through them, representing the Nile.'

'We're a long way from Egypt,' Gemma said.

Inside, the corridor stretched ahead of them, the walls narrowing into a tunnel-like passage. The air grew cooler, the heat from the jungle replaced by a bone-deep chill that seeped into their bones. The ground was smooth, as if worn down over thousands of years. Every sound echoed off the structure, from the soft padding of Kitty Stardust's paws to the heavy thud of Callisto's footsteps.

Tension gripped Ella as they pressed deeper into the pyramid. The air stank of decay, the pungent scent of ancient, forgotten things long buried in the darkness. She touched the walls, fingers tracing the strange symbols carved into the stone. There was a sense of power, something old and dangerous lurking beneath the surface.

'This place... it's not like anything I've ever seen,' Andrew murmured, his voice hushed, almost reverent. His eyes roved over the hieroglyphics that lined the walls, studying them with the same intensity he used when conducting an experiment. 'These symbols don't match any known language on Earth, but there are similarities.'

'Similarities to what?' Ella asked.

'Ancient cultures,' Gemma chimed in. 'The Egyptians, the Sumerians, the Mayans. They all had legends of gods that came from the sky, powerful beings who shaped the world. This could be connected.'

Seraphina nodded. 'The Elementals have been part of Earth's history for far longer than humans have known. But what concerns me is the connection to The Soulless. The symbols on this pyramid speak of creation, destruction, and something that lurks in the spaces between.'

As they continued, the corridor opened into a large chamber. Intricate carvings covered the walls, depicting scenes of battle, of gods and monsters locked in eternal conflict. In the centre lay rows of stone sarcophagi, each adorned with an ornate, golden mask. The faces of the mummies beneath the masks were obscured, but Ella sensed their presence, like ghosts lingering just out of sight.

The room stank of dust and rot, the ancient scent of death that had settled there long ago. The mummies, preserved in their golden sarcophagi, were a testament to the advanced knowledge of whoever had built the place. There was a quiet reverence in how the others moved through the chamber; their voices lowered as if intruding on some sacred burial ground.

Delf lingered near one sarcophagus, studying the carvings. 'These hieroglyphs tell the story of an ancient civilisation long before recorded human history. They speak of when the gods walked the Earth, when the world was young and full of magic. But there's something else, something darker.'

Kitty Stardust, who had been sniffing around the edge

of the room, growled low in her throat. 'I feel it, too. Something's wrong here.'

'Look at this,' Andrew said, pointing to a wall section where the carvings seemed to shift as if telling a different story. 'These figures—they're not human. And the symbols match the ones on the pyramid's exterior.'

Ella squinted at them. The beings were tall and gaunt, their eyes glowing with a malevolent light. They held weapons that crackled with energy, and behind them, great darkness loomed, swirling with tendrils of shadow.

'Are those Elementals?' she asked.

'No,' Seraphina whispered. 'That's The Soulless. This place is a shrine to them.'

Before Ella could process that, there was a faint hum, barely audible at first but growing louder by the second. The ground trembled, and the air crackled with energy. The light in the room dimmed, casting eerie shadows across the walls.

'Everyone, stay alert,' Barbara warned, gripping the hilt of her sword.

Without warning, the sarcophagi stirred. The lids slid open with a grating sound, and the mummified figures inside rose. But they weren't ordinary mummies. Their golden masks gleamed in the gloom as they stood, and their eyes flickered with an unnatural, bluish light. They moved with a strange, mechanical precision, joints clicking and whirring like machines.

'Robots?' Ella gasped, stepping back as a figure lurched towards them.

'More like guardians,' Delf corrected. 'Placed here to protect something.'

Before anyone could react, the first of the robotic mummies lunged. Callisto roared, charging forward with a speed that belied her massive form. Her claws slashed through the air, meeting the metal body of the mummy with a resounding clang. Sparks flew, but the creature didn't falter.

'Move!' Barbara shouted, drawing her sword and cutting down another approaching mummy.

The room erupted into chaos. Ella ducked as one mummy swung a metallic arm at her, the wind from its attack ruffling her hair. Seraphina used the light in her palm to create a blast, forcing a creature to crash into the wall, but more kept coming.

'They're not stopping!' Andrew yelled, pulling Gemma behind him as more mummies advanced on them.

'They're protecting something!' Seraphina shouted, her eyes darting around the room, searching for the source of their aggression. 'We need to find out what!'

Ella's heart throbbed as she dodged an attack. Her gaze flicked to the chamber's centre, where a raised stone platform stood. Atop it, illuminated by the faint blue glow of the hieroglyphs, was an object—a small idol carved from some dark, unknown material. Its surface was etched with the same swirling symbols that covered the walls, and at its base, a strange carving pulsed with energy.

'That's it!' Ella yelled, pointing to the object. 'That's what they're protecting!'

Seraphina's eyes widened as she saw it. 'It's the Idol of The Soulless. Everyone, stop! We can't let it be touched.'

But it was too late. In the heat of the moment, Ella rushed toward the plinth. Her fingers brushed the surface of the idol before Seraphina's warning could sink in. A blast of energy surged through her, far more intense than anything she'd felt before. Everything went still, as if frozen in time.

Then, a blinding beam of light shot out from the idol,

engulfing the chamber. Ella tried to scream, to pull away, but she couldn't move. The light wrapped around her, pulling her in, until everything else—the room, the robotic mummies, her parents and friends—faded.

There was a sound, like the tearing of fabric, and the place shifted. The ground gave way, and Ella felt like she was falling through space, the light consuming her. Her body became weightless, her mind spinning as the world dissolved into a swirl of colour and sensation. Voices echoed in the distance, but she couldn't make out the words. The light pulsed, growing brighter and brighter until it became unbearable. Just when she thought she could take no more, it vanished as quickly as it had come.

Ella blinked, gasping for breath. She was no longer in the pyramid. Around her, the landscape had changed. She stood in the middle of a barren wasteland, the sky a swirling mass of dark clouds. The ground was cracked and dry, devoid of life. In the distance, jagged mountains loomed, their peaks shrouded in mist. The air was heavy and thick with the scent of ash and decay.

The others were there too—her parents, Seraphina, Delf, Barbara, and the rest of the group—scattered around her, all looking disoriented.

'What... what happened?' Gemma stammered.

Seraphina's face was pale, her eyes filled with dread. 'We've been transported,' she said. 'This is their realm. The Soulless.'

Ella's heart sank as those words settled over them. The Idol had been a trap, a doorway to something far worse than they could have imagined.

And now, they were right in the middle of it.

Then, someone grabbed her shoulder.

Chapter 9

Stonehenge

A bright star flashed before Ella's eyes before everything went dark.

Then she saw through the light, turning to see her father behind her.

'What happened?' she said.

'I heard Seraphina shouting before you touched the stone,' Andrew Finn answered.

Ella stared at him. 'I didn't hear her.' She glanced around to see they were outside alone. 'Where are the others?'

'I don't know.'

Panic gripped her. 'Don't you remember? We were in the realm of The Soulless.'

He shook his head. 'No. We were in the pyramid fighting those mummy things, and the next thing I know, we're here.'

She peered at her fingers, still sensing the touch of the stone. 'I think it transported us here. It had the same feeling I got when I travelled through the multiverse.'

'Do you think that's where we are?'

She shrugged. 'I'm not sure.' Ella peered at the monument in the distance. 'That looks like Stonehenge, but different.'

It smelt of summer, and the sun was low in the sky. She shielded her eyes from its gaze and steadied her beating heart. The stone circle was impressive even from where they stood, but she knew it wasn't the place she'd visited on a school trip. Yet, somehow, she was confident they hadn't stepped into the multiverse.

So, where was this version of Stonehenge?

Her father grimaced. 'Can you hear that?'

She moved closer to him, unsure of what he meant until she heard what she thought was chanting nearby. Then she saw the mass of people striding towards the stones, singing as they went. There must have been forty or fifty men, women, and children. They marched across the ground in two columns, with the second set carrying what looked like piles of clothes on stretchers until Ella realised they weren't clothes. She grabbed her father and dragged him back. There was no shelter where they were, no bushes or trees, only open grassland and a slight slope. But it made no difference to those approaching the stone, as they paid no heed to Ella or her father.

'Maybe we should leave,' he said, gripping her hand.

She shook her head. 'They're no danger to us, Pop.'

He narrowed his eyes at her. 'Since when do you call me that?'

She shrugged. 'In light of what's transpired to us, it seemed appropriate.'

Ella kept her focus on the group as he spoke. 'So you know what happened when you touched that stone?'

'We're at Stonehenge.'

'Yes, Ella, I realise that. But there's something else, isn't there?'

Some people glanced at her as they went past, mainly the children, but they continued to chant as they approached the giant stones.

'Somehow, that relic popped us back in time, perhaps four or five thousand years, and now we're watching a funeral ceremony.'

Andrew Finn sighed, let go of his daughter, and sat. As she looked at him, he appeared to have the weight of the world on his shoulders. 'How do you know this, Ella?'

She joined him. 'Look at the condition of the stones. Even from here, they seem pristine compared to my last visit. And some are in different positions. So, that rules out us being in our time. It must be in the past, in the early days of Stonehenge.'

He smiled at her. 'You have a good eye, but how do you know that's a funeral?'

Ella nodded. 'This Neolithic road was constructed at the same time as Stonehenge, and it lines up with the sun on the shortest day of the year. Researchers have suggested Stonehenge was part of a ritual landscape, a domain of the dead. A journey along the Avon to reach Stonehenge was part of a sacred passage from life to death to celebrate past ancestors and the deceased. That must be what we're witnessing.'

His grin grew large enough to cover his face. 'And how do you know all this?'

She stood, and he followed. 'I've watched loads of the Discovery Channel this year.'

The smile slipped from him. 'Since you returned from the multiverse?'

'I've always been curious, Pop.'

He shook his head. 'Okay, you can cut that out. This whole situation is weird enough without you calling me silly names.' The chanting increased as the group entered the stones. 'Do you think you accidentally transported us here using your abilities?'

'No, this has nothing to do with me.' She didn't know how she knew that, but she was sure. When she'd explained about the Light inside her, Ella's mother theorised it was an unknown energy, probably from another dimension. Her father had suggested running a few experiments, but Gemma Finn was adamant her daughter wouldn't be a lab rat.

So, they'd accepted how special she was but spoke little about it.

'Then why would the stone send us here, and what's happened to the others?'

Ella didn't know. She pointed at the group's last member, who was disappearing into Stonehenge. 'Maybe we'll find the answer in there.'

'Do you think it's safe?'

'If we keep our distance, we should be okay.'

He grabbed her hand. 'Are you worried about your mother and the others?'

She thought of what she'd seen in The Soulless realm. 'No. Maybe I saw something that might happen because of my connection to the Book of All Life, or perhaps it was an aftereffect from my previous vision.'

They strode towards the outer ring of stones. She may have sounded casual when telling him they'd likely travelled back over four thousand years, but what had happened made every inch of her tremble. She kept calm as they stepped inside and stared at the group.

'Do you remember your grandmother's funeral?'

She only had a hazy recollection of it. She was five when Ruth, her father's mother, passed away. 'I remember how upset you and Mum were.'

He gripped her fingers. 'Grief is terrible, Ella, and everyone deals with it in their own way.' The sadness in his eyes melted her heart. 'But as long as we keep the memories of those we've lost with us, they'll never be forgotten.' He let go of her and gazed at the people as the chanting stopped.

'The dead don't bury themselves,' she said. Her father stared at her. 'I heard someone say that on TV. Like you said, they'll always be with us no matter what.' She nodded towards the group as they lowered the bodies into a large hole in the ground. 'And ceremonies like this play a huge part in that, as well as allowing the living to pay their respects.'

She remembered the dirt she'd thrown on her grandmother's coffin and how the cemetery was covered in a blanket of peace and calm. Her parents hadn't cried then, but she'd heard them sobbing in the following days and weeks.

She should have been thinking about how they would return to the island but was fascinated by the ceremony. Once several bodies were lowered into the ground, the rest of the adults constructed a burial mound. All apart from one man, who moved towards the inner circle of bluestones. He removed a long piece of wood from his robe and struck the closest bluestone. It responded with a loud clanging sound, which reverberated around Stonehenge. He repeated the process on other stones until it was as if she was inside a cathedral of sound. The women and children chanted again, creating a harmonious noise alongside the ringing rocks.

'Do you know why they've done that?' her father said.

She did. 'In certain ancient cultures, rocks that ring out were believed to contain mystic or healing powers. Stonehenge has a history of association with rituals and as a place for rejuvenation.'

'You think they're trying to resurrect the dead?'

She shook her head. 'No, I believe this has more to do with the living, of healing anything emotional or physical which might harm them.'

Andrew Finn grinned. 'When did my daughter become so insightful?'

'I've always been clever, Dad, you know that. I get it from you and Mum.'

The sun started disappearing over the horizon, and darkness fell across his face. 'But now you're much more than that, with this Light inside you.'

She wondered if the ceremony they were observing had reawakened his curiosity about her. 'All living things have Light in them, Dad. It's just stronger in me.'

'And this is because of the Elementals and that book you're connected to?'

When she'd explained to her parents about the Book of All Life and the Elemental realm, she'd left out some more significant facts, including how Pandora claimed to be Ella's ancestor and the Creator of everything. Not that she wanted to hide anything from them, but with Pandora's abduction of them and their subsequent memory loss, she'd thought it better not to overwhelm them with too much information at once, especially about the revelation connecting the so-called family lineage between Pandora and Ella and her mother.

She'd explained the concept of Light as best she could, unsurprised her mother identified it as energy and not as something as mystical as the Soul. Her parents weren't atheists but weren't religious, driven by science. She spent considerable time telling them about her adventures in the multiverse, which she knew they could explain scientifically, rather than pondering an all-powerful God who'd created everything and who they were related to. The idea gave her a headache, and she didn't want to put them under a similar strain.

So Ella had told them what she thought they needed to know so they wouldn't believe she'd lost her mind. And that's why she'd said her connection was to the Book, not to Pandora. She'd need to tell them the truth one day, but this wasn't it.

'Yes, the Book of All Life allows me to bring Elementals into our world and they can share their Light with me, and vice versa, and we both get stronger because of it.'

He nodded. 'Like a symbiosis. Your mother and I spoke about this.'

She watched his face darken as the sun vanished and the ceremony ended. The living marched out of the stones once the burial mound was completed, with only a few shooting cursory glances at them. Ella had read that people had come from all over Europe to Stonehenge thousands of years before it became a tourist attraction. She assumed this group was used to having observers at their ceremonies.

They left, and silence filled the stones. She touched her chest, glad to have witnessed the ceremony, but they were no further forward in finding a way back to the island and their correct place in time. Her father must have been reading her mind.

'So what do we do now?'

Ella considered removing the Book from her backpack and maybe using it to return home, but dismissed the idea. They needed more information first.

She stared into the surrounding emptiness. 'There must be a reason we were brought here. It can't have been random. Can it?'

As she pondered that, a hooded figure stepped from behind an inner stone and strode towards them. Ella tensed her legs, ready for defensive action, but relaxed when the hood was removed to reveal a teenage girl not much older than her.

'Why are you here, outlanders?'

'We don't know,' Andrew Finn said.

'How can we understand you?' They may have been standing inside Stonehenge, but she doubted the girl spoke the same version of English as they did.

Her blue eyes sparkled. 'The children of the Chosen are capable of many things.' She gazed at Ella. 'I sense the same about you, child.'

'Who are you?' Ella said.

'I am Lyssa, guardian of the sacred stone.'

Ella's father pointed at the blocks of Stonehenge. 'Aren't these sacred?'

'None of these are the sacred stone the Chosen are tasked to protect.'

A thought gripped Ella. 'Is there a carving of a winged creature with a demon's face on this sacred stone?'

Lyssa's expression turned as dark as the sky. 'What of it?'

Ella moved toward her. 'That's how we got here. I touched a stone like that, and we were transported through time and space.'

'Time and space?' Lyssa asked.

'Yes, I don't know how it works, but maybe your sacred stone could send us back.'

The excitement surged through her so much she

couldn't help but grab at Lyssa. As Ella reached for her, the other girl vanished.

'What?' Andrew Finn asked.

Before Ella could reply, Lyssa reappeared behind them. She placed a hand on father and daughter, and all three disappeared.

Chapter 10

Giza

The light scorched Seraphina's face so much she had to lift her arms for protection. She stumbled to the side as the ringing in her ears punched into her skull. The illumination and the others were gone when she took her arms away. Sand was underneath her feet, the desert surrounding her as she realised she was no longer on the island. The air was clean, untouched by pollution, and the sky was as blue as a clear sea. She clenched her hands into fists as someone approached her from behind.

'That stone transported us here.'

Seraphina turned to see Callisto. 'Did you see what was carved into it?'

Callisto rubbed at her stomach as it growled. 'Yes, it was a winged creature, clawed on hands and feet and the most unpleasant face. I've seen nothing like it in my long life, either on Earth or in the Elemental world. Have you?'

Seraphina shook her head. 'Where do you think we are?'

Callisto lifted one hairy arm and pointed over Seraphina's shoulder. 'That structure in the distance looks familiar.'

Seraphina stared at what she meant, unable to distinguish what it was beyond a large building reaching into the clouds. Then, as she strained her eyes, it became clearer, and she realised what it was: a pyramid.

'Are we outside where we were, and are the others still inside?' Her heart beat faster as she worried about them, especially Ella, even though she knew the child was gifted with extraordinary abilities.

Callisto's guts continued to rumble. 'No, that's not the pyramid where we were. It's much more famous than that, and there's more than one.'

Seraphina focused her vision until she recognised where they were. 'We're in Egypt?'

'I guess so,' Callisto said. 'Though I'm more interested in when we are than where.'

'What do you mean?'

Callisto raised two enormous arms in the air. 'Don't you feel it, my friend, the difference in the atmosphere? I think we've travelled through time, but for why, I don't know.'

Seraphina strode towards the pyramids. 'Then let's find out.'

The bear walked next to her. 'Have you travelled through time before?'

Seraphina laughed. 'No, I didn't realise it was possible.'

Callisto's strides were longer than Seraphina's, so she slowed her pace not to get ahead. 'I never thanked you for rescuing me from that Institute prison.'

'There's no need,' Seraphina said. She stopped to wipe the sweat from her head. 'It looks like we have at least an hour's walk.'

The bear's stomach grumbled again. 'Of course, and let's hope there are people with food when we arrive.'

Seraphina's throat was as dry as the sand they marched

across. 'And water as well.' She lifted her hand. 'My Light also appears to have dried up. How do you feel? Are your guts rumbling because of fear?'

Callisto's laugh was long and loud. 'I am the daughter of Lycaon, a terrible and vicious man. His deeds were so dreadful the gods changed him into a wolf, and he became the first of the werewolves. Nothing scares me.' She grinned. 'But I am hungry.'

Seraphina nodded. 'I hunted a pack of werewolves in the north of England a few years ago, and it wasn't pretty.'

'They must still contain my father's genes,' Callisto said. 'I preferred the woods to his company. I loved to hunt and became friends with Artemis, joining her band of nymphs and swearing to stay free forever. As one of her group, I'd never have to marry a man of my father's choosing and could remain without domestic responsibilities in the forest my whole life.' She sighed as they approached the pyramids. 'Like many beautiful nymphs, I caught the eye of Zeus, who disguised himself as Artemis.'

Seraphina glanced into Callisto's face, spotting the woman behind the bear's eyes. 'You and Artemis were a couple?'

'We loved each other,' Callisto said. 'And Zeus used that love to trick me into his embrace. I couldn't break free from him when he'd revealed his true self.' They walked on in silence. As the pyramids appeared a few yards away, Callisto continued. 'Nine months later, I gave birth to a boy. For that, Zeus's wife, Hera, turned me into a bear and took my child, Arcas, from me.'

The shadow of the Great Pyramid of Giza fell upon them.

'Your son is out there somewhere, Callisto. I'll help you find him when we sort whatever this is.'

They stopped at the foot of the structure. 'Thank you, Seraphina.'

Callisto's stomach rumbled again.

Seraphina changed the conversation and stared beyond the pyramid. 'It looks like a market over there where we can get you something to eat.'

Callisto laughed. 'And how will you explain me to the locals?'

'Simple. I'll say you're my pet.'

The bear, once a woman, growled as they headed towards the marketplace. Seraphina smelt the food before they arrived as the aroma of cooked meats and baked bread drifted towards her. Sellers stood behind their stalls as the public perused their wares. Seraphina saw vendors selling medicines, amulets, jewellery, perfumes, clothing, fruit, vegetables and all kinds of food, leather and wooden goods, papyrus and ink, live animals, dead animals, tools, rugs, furniture, and salt. They all stopped what they were doing to stare at her and Callisto.

'Perhaps this wasn't such a good idea,' the bear whispered to her.

Seraphina thought the same before the hush turned into a noisy marketplace again, as if seeing a seven-foot bear was an everyday occurrence. Then there was Seraphina in her strange clothes and shoes. But the Egyptians continued with their business as Callisto led Seraphina to a giant pan of sizzling meat. She moved one hairy hand towards it.

'That will do for me.'

Seraphina nodded. 'Okay.' She stepped up to the table and smiled at the woman behind it before pointing at the food and rubbing her stomach. 'I hope she understands this.'

The woman must have done as she grabbed a large

spoon and scooped a generous portion of meat and vegetables into a pot.

Callisto licked her lips. 'How will you pay for it?'

'That's a good question,' Seraphina replied, 'but ancient Egypt used a bartering system for goods and services.'

The bear took the food from the woman. 'And what do you have to barter with, my friend?' She used her clawed fingers to scoop a generous portion into her mouth, and Seraphina also realised she was hungry.

Seraphina pointed at her chest and then the food. 'Can I have one more, please?' She knew the woman wouldn't understand the words but hoped she'd get the drift from the tone, which she did as she served another helping. Seraphina took it, the heat warming her fingers as she held it. That's when the woman pointed at Seraphina's wrist.

'She wants your mechanical timepiece,' Callisto said through a mouthful of meat.

Seraphina put down the bowl, removed her watch, and handed it to the woman. Then she retrieved her meal and walked away with Callisto. 'If we sit at the feet of the Sphinx and eat, I hope it doesn't offend our hosts.'

'Aren't you worried you might change history by giving her your timepiece?'

Seraphina laughed. 'Do you want me to return your food to her?'

The bear scrunched her eyes. 'Oh no, history can go to rot, my friend. My belly is much more important.'

They sat in the shade of the Sphinx and ate in silence, observing the locals at the marketplace. Callisto's stomach stopped rumbling as Seraphina tasted a cavalcade of spices. Seraphina might have appreciated their unique situation if things hadn't been so dire. She licked her lips, finished her meal, and put the bowl on the ground.

'So, what do we do next?'

Callisto smiled at her. 'I've told you the story of my life, so now it's your turn.'

'Do you know the history of witches?'

'No,' Callisto replied.

Seraphina grinned. 'Well, you're in for a treat.'

She adjusted her position, leaning against the ancient foot of the Sphinx. She glanced at its worn face, weathered by centuries of wind and sand, and felt a strange connection to it. Something timeless, unchanging, while everything else seemed in constant flux.

Callisto wiped her mouth, the last bits of food gone. 'Well?' The bear's eyes twinkled with curiosity. 'I'm waiting for this history lesson.'

Seraphina chuckled. 'All right, but it's not a pleasant story. Witches... we've always been feared. Misunderstood. You see, magic isn't something that's chosen. It awakens within certain people at a young age. It comes from Light, but it's different. It's wild at first, unpredictable. And for centuries, those who showed signs of it were hunted, tortured, or killed.'

Callisto's face darkened. 'Fear of the unknown. It always leads to the same thing.'

Seraphina nodded. 'In the early days, witches were solitary, keeping their abilities hidden, but eventually, covens formed. Groups of witches, mostly women, who found safety in numbers. They shared knowledge, taught each other how to control their powers, and protected one another. That's when the real persecution began. The more organised we became, the more the Church and others saw us as a threat.'

'I assume it didn't end well for many.'

Seraphina sighed, her eyes clouding with memories.

'No, it didn't. The witch hunts swept across Europe and the colonies in the Americas. Thousands of women—and men —were accused of witchcraft and killed. And the worst part? Most of them weren't even witches. Just ordinary people who were unlucky enough to be caught in the hysteria.'

Callisto growled, her claws digging into the sand. 'The cruelty of humans never ceases to amaze me.'

'Cruelty and fear go hand in hand,' Seraphina said. 'But witches survived. We adapted and went deeper into hiding, masking our powers or using them secretly. Over time, we became something of legend. Now, in the modern world, most people don't believe in witches at all. It's easier for us that way.'

Callisto studied her, her large head tilted to the side. 'But you... you're different, aren't you? You don't hide.'

Seraphina smiled, though there was a sadness behind it. 'I don't have that luxury. My family was one of the old covens, and our lineage stretches back to the first witches. We hold the knowledge of generations, and with that comes responsibility. I can't just disappear and live in the shadows.'

Callisto nodded. 'And what of your family now?'

Seraphina hesitated, her eyes flickering with pain. 'They're gone. Most of them, anyway. The humans took them. My sister... she fought beside me until the end. She was my last connection to the old ways.'

'I'm sorry,' Callisto said. 'Losing family is something I understand all too well.'

Seraphina nodded, her throat tight. 'I've been alone ever since. Until now.'

They sat for a moment, the sounds of the marketplace buzzing in the distance. The sun's heat had lessened as it dipped toward the horizon, casting long shadows across the desert.

'So, what's the plan?' Callisto asked, breaking the silence. 'We've eaten, rested... but we're still stranded here. Wherever—or whenever—here is.'

Seraphina glanced around, her mind working through the possibilities. 'I'm not sure. If we've been transported through time, there has to be a reason for it. Magic doesn't work randomly, especially not magic as powerful as what brought us here.'

Callisto grunted. 'That stone, the one with the strange carving. It felt like old magic. Ancient, even by my standards.'

Seraphina frowned. 'Yes, but why here? Why Egypt? And why now? And where are the others?'

Before Callisto could answer, a low, distant rumble caught Seraphina's attention. She turned her head toward the horizon, where the pyramids loomed large and imposing. The noise intensified, vibrating through the ground beneath them.

'What is that?' Callisto asked, standing for a better view.

Seraphina stood as well, her eyes narrowing as the rumbling grew closer. It wasn't just the sound—there was a feeling, too. A shift in the air, a subtle pulse of energy, made her skin tingle. Then, a group of figures on horses appeared behind one of the smaller pyramids, moving toward them. At first, they were mere silhouettes against the orange glow of the setting sun, but as they neared, Seraphina could make out their forms more clearly.

They were soldiers dressed in armour that glinted in the fading light. At the head of the group was a tall figure cloaked in dark robes, his face obscured by a hood. His presence exuded authority and power, and the energy in the air intensified as he approached.

'Who are they?' Callisto growled, ready to defend herself.

Seraphina didn't answer. Her eyes were locked on the figure in the robes.

The group stopped a few paces away, and the hooded man forced his steed forward, his voice low and commanding. 'You are out of place here.'

Seraphina's hand went to the hilt of her dagger, her muscles tensing. 'We didn't come here by choice. Who are you?'

He pulled back his hood, revealing a gaunt, pale face with sharp features and piercing eyes. He studied them for a long moment. 'I am the Guardian of the Pharaoh's Secrets. You have trespassed in a time that does not belong to you.'

Callisto growled, but Seraphina held up a hand to stop her. 'We touched a stone and were brought here by magic. We didn't mean to trespass. We're just trying to figure out what's going on.'

His eyes narrowed. 'Magic? There's no magic here that you can control, witch.'

The word hung like a blade, and she felt her pulse quicken. He knew what she was. That wasn't good.

'What do you want from us?' she asked, steadying her voice.

His lips curled into a cold smile. 'The magic that brought you here is not of your making. It is tied to the ancient forces that guard this land. Forces you have disturbed.'

Seraphina exchanged a glance with Callisto. The stone and carving had all felt wrong, as if they'd triggered something far older and more powerful than they understood.

'We didn't mean to disturb anything,' she said. 'If you let us go, we'll leave and never return.'

The Guardian shook his head. 'It's not that simple. The moment you touched that stone, you became part of the story. And now, there is no going back.'

Seraphina's grip tightened on her dagger. 'What do you mean?'

The Guardian's eyes gleamed with a strange, unnatural light. 'You are here to fulfil a prophecy. One that has been written in the sands of time for millennia.'

Callisto let out a huff of disbelief. 'Prophecies. Always with the prophecies.'

Seraphina ignored her, focusing on the Guardian. 'What prophecy?'

'The return of the Warden of Souls,' he said, his voice dropping to a whisper. 'And the end of the old gods.'

Seraphina's breath caught in her throat. The Warden of Souls was a name she hadn't heard in a long time. It was a legend, a myth among witches—a figure of unimaginable power who held dominion over life and death.

'This can't be right,' she murmured. 'The Warden of Souls is just a story.'

His smile widened. 'All stories have roots in truth, witch. And you are part of that truth.'

Seraphina shivered. She had been dragged into something far bigger than herself, and its weight pressed on her shoulders. 'What happens now?'

His eyes gleamed. 'You must choose. Fulfil the prophecy or be destroyed by it.'

Chapter 11

Kitty and Peg

Kitty Stardust fell fifty feet and landed on her paws. Her claws gripped the grass as she examined her surroundings: she was outside, and the smell of the river was in the air. When she confirmed she was alone, Kitty spoke to the friend only she could see.

'I guess we're not in Kansas anymore, Lulu.'

What are you on about? a voice whispered in her ear.

'This isn't our little island hideaway. We're not inside that pyramid, and our friends aren't here.'

Is that why you're talking to me because they can't see you making a fool of yourself?

She ignored the insult and stared at the buildings, rows of houses standing next to a structure pumping out smoke at an industrial rate. A scattering of crows sped from the city as the smell of burning wood drifted into her lungs. A child's doll lay broken on the pavement.

Now's your chance to escape and find our way home.

Kitty stared at the smoke, unsure if it was a building on fire or a factory working at peak production.

'We won't get home on our own, Lulu. How long did we

try that and achieve nothing? But I'm sure Ella and the others will help us if we can find them.'

I don't trust the girl or the witch. One has too much Light, and the other craves it unnaturally. Wherever we are now, it's better than with them.

Kitty gazed at the buildings. 'I think we're in London. That's St Paul's Cathedral over there, but the skyline looks different from when the Institute dumped me in a cell.' She scratched at her arm as a tingle ran through it. 'And if it weren't for Seraphina, we'd still be imprisoned there.'

Why don't you tell them about me if you trust them so much?

Kitty sighed. 'And what would I say? I fell through a hole in my world to end up in a different one, and when I woke up, you whispered to me. I'm sure they'd be impressed by that.'

You think you're mad, and I'm not real, but the only madness is not realising I've always been inside you. The trip between realms brought me out, and you've been so much better since, haven't you? I don't know why you won't admit it.

Kitty pulled a clump of hair from her arm and dropped it into the grass.

'We'll talk about it later. Let's try to find Ella and the others.'

Lulu grumbled in Kitty's ear as the talking cat approached the smoke. The night engulfed her as she reached the first row of houses, moving along the back behind clothes hanging on a washing line. No one was there, so she grabbed a damp shawl and wrapped it around her shoulders and face. The dark should conceal her non-human appearance, and she had something to hide her head.

Once a thief, always a thief.

'If the locals kill me because I'm a six-foot talking cat, that means the end of you as well, Lulu.'

Kitty wouldn't admit it, but she was concerned as she entered the city. The Institute had kept her imprisoned for five years there - five years of eating cold food and sleeping on a straw pallet in a damp cell, a time without fondness, kindness, or love, five long years when her only companion was Lulu.

She pushed the memories away as she stepped into the street, and even with the shawl clutched to her face, she could smell the smoke. She noticed a crowd gazing at a house in flames. People shouted for the fire engines, but Kitty only heard the screams from inside the building, the howls of the trapped coming over the fire crackling in the air.

Some people tried to push inside, but the heat and the smoke forced them back.

We should leave, Kitty. If someone sees who you are, a panicked mob will blame you for this tragedy.

Lulu might have been right, but the blaze mesmerised Kitty. Her instincts screamed at her to flee, to run as far away as possible, but something made her stay.

The fire grew so large it turned the night sky into shimmering shades of red and yellow. The crowd increased around her, with some falling to their knees in prayer. A child's voice was heard inside the house, and Kitty's heart was close to melting.

Then, an incredible thing happened.

A figure staggered out of the blaze. Smoke clung to her frame, but not the two young children she carried. She stumbled towards the crowd as two women, the children's mothers, Kitty assumed, rushed to the rescuer. They grabbed the kids as the woman stepped away from the flames, and Kitty recognised that flowing green hair trailing behind her.

'Peg,' she shouted as she ran to the hero of the night. Kitty threw her arms around Peg Powler and hugged the life from her. When she let go, her clothes were damp. 'How did you do that?'

The emerald hue of her eyes matched the hair resting on her shoulders. 'I'm a water sprite, Kitty. Fire can't harm me.'

A horse-drawn fire engine arrived as Kitty dragged Peg from the crowd. 'How did you end up in that building?'

Peg shook her head. 'I have no idea. The last thing I remember is being in the pyramid as Ella reached for that stone. A bright light blinded me, and when I could see again, I was inside that inferno, with the children crying on the floor above me. I climbed the stairs before they cracked, grabbed the kids, and you know the rest.'

Kitty took a deep breath. 'You were in a cell near me at the Institute.'

'How did you know?' Peg asked.

'The guards would talk about the other inmates, the monsters, they called them.'

Peg Powler's green eyes sparkled. 'What do you think, Kitty Stardust?'

'I think we should get out of here.'

'And go where?'

'Our options are limited,' Kitty replied. 'This is not the time we came from.' She watched as the firefighters pumped water into the blaze. 'This looks like Victorian London.'

'That stone sent us back in time,' Peg said. 'I've heard of such things.'

'You have?'

'Yes, they're a rune stone. Did you see the carving of the creature on it?'

'A winged beast with claws.'

'A true monster.' Peg peered at the crowd as they gazed at the flames. 'Nothing good will come from this.'

'I agree, but what should we do?'

Find somewhere with no humans, Lulu whispered in her ear.

'We need to locate a mage,' Peg answered. 'Only a mystic can return us to our time.' She gazed into the sky. 'Let's head towards the river; there's one over there.'

She set off, and Kitty scampered next to her. 'How do you know that?'

Peg tapped her nose. 'It's simple, my friend. I can smell magic a mile away.'

They left the fire and turned into the nearby street, Kitty striding by Peg's side. The sound of pumping water disappeared as they entered a slum smelling of the worst excesses of humanity. They skirted the desperate bodies begging for food and stuck to the shadows. Peg's long green hair flowed behind her as an icy wind struck and bit at the shawl covering most of Kitty's face. Kitty pulled it down a little to speak without getting bits of cotton in her mouth.

'I should have brought my notebook with me.'

'Do you want to keep a record of our journey through history?'

Kitty laughed. 'No. Walking down these streets is giving me an idea for a song.'

Peg's eyes blazed under the moonlight. 'You're a singer?'

She nodded. 'Before the Institute abducted me, I had my band, Kitty Stardust and the Comets.' She removed the cover from her head and carried it in one hand. 'I wonder if they've replaced me by now.'

Peggy stopped in front of a house at the end of the street. It stood separate from the others, twice the size, and as immaculate as those were weather-beaten and falling apart.

'When we return, you'll sing for Ella and the rest of the group. Do you think you can keep your song simmering until then?'

'I guess I'll have to.' She stared at the entrance. 'Is the mage inside there?'

'That's what my nose tells me.' Peg strode up the steps and knocked on the door.

What's the plan? Lulu said in Kitty's mind.

'What's the plan?' Kitty repeated.

The door creaked open before Peg could reply. Kitty covered her head, exposing only her eyes. Standing there was an old woman with thin arms but an ample middle concealed by a long, dark dress. Her hollow face remained indifferent to the visitors on the doorstep.

Peg started to speak, but the woman stopped her with a raised crooked finger.

'He knows why you're here. Close the door behind you and follow me.'

She took them upstairs and into a bedroom occupied by a bed of heroic proportions. They saw a large man wearing balaclava and mittens, almost obscured by bedclothes, flanked by cases containing figurines and ornaments. Mahogany cabinets displayed hundreds of antique jewels.

Peg's nose twitched, and Kitty inhaled the mixed aroma of dusty papers and strange chemicals. A fire crackled at the back, reminding Kitty of the burning house where she'd been reunited with Peg. She watched the flames dance in the grate, wincing as they lapped towards the ceiling. She glimpsed Lulu in the blaze, taunting her with accusations of weakness.

You should tell her you learnt to play the guitar in prison and why you were there.

Lulu's voice lived in her head, but it was the faces of the dead she saw in the flames as they burnt as red as an exploding sun.

'Remove the cloth from your face,' the man said after the woman left the room.

Kitty hesitated until Peg nodded at her. His eyes never left her as she removed the shawl. She expected him to gasp when he saw her, but he only grinned as she dropped the cloth on the floor.

'Who are you?' Kitty asked.

The bed sheets rippled as if they were the top of a lake, and something monstrous lingered beneath it. 'My name is Dr John Dee, and you're from another world, but your friend is a supernatural creature.'

'How do you know this?' Peg said.

'The angels tell me everything. They know who you are and where you're from.'

Kitty moved closer to the bed. 'Can you help us return home?' She didn't consider the island her home, but her friends were her new family.

Dee lifted a withered hand. 'I'm incapable of visiting the toilet without assistance, so returning you two to your future time is impossible, I'm afraid.'

Kitty puffed out her cheeks and slumped into a chair nearby.

Peg turned to her. 'How long do talking cats live for?'

'What year is this?' Kitty asked.

'1899,' Dee replied.

Kitty put her head in her hands. 'I won't live long enough to see the twenty-first century.' She peered at Dee. 'Are you sure there's nothing you can do for us?'

His aged eyes gazed deep into her. 'Only one thing can help you, but I don't have it.'

Kitty jumped from the chair. 'What is it?'

A cold wisp of air drifted from his mouth as he spoke. 'Have you heard of the *Necronomicon*?'

She shook her head, but Peg replied.

'The Book of the Dead can help us?'

The old man nodded. 'There is a spell in there I will use to send you home, but I don't have the book anymore, as someone stole it from me.'

'Where is it?' Kitty asked.

Dee grinned at her. 'Are you a cat thief?'

'I'll get the book,' she said. 'Just tell us where it is.'

His crooked smile revealed yellowed teeth.

'You'll need to steal it from Crowley.'

Chapter 12

Pumapunku

Gemma was falling, tumbling through space and time, weightless as the world around her dissolved into a blur of light and shadow. Barbara felt the rush of wind against her skin, the sensation of being pulled in every direction at once. Delf was between them, reaching out and trying to use his magic to slow their fall.

But nothing happened.

Then they slammed into solid earth.

Barbara gasped as she hit the earth, her legs buckling beneath her. She fell to her knees, the taste of dust and dry air filling her mouth. The ground was hard, radiating a strange, primal energy. She looked up, her eyes adjusting to the harsh, golden sunlight that bathed everything in a surreal glow.

They'd landed in the middle of a vast, ancient ruin.

'What happened?' Gemma asked as Barbara helped her up.

'Ella opened a portal when she touched that stone,' the Valkyrie answered. 'We've travelled somewhere, but I don't recognise this place.'

'Pumapunku,' Delf replied. 'I've been here before.'

Gemma looked around them. 'Where are Ella and the others?'

Barbara scrutinised their surroundings. 'I don't know. Maybe they're in these ruins.'

Pumapunku stretched out before them, a labyrinth of massive stone blocks, precision-carved and aligned despite their immense size. Everything felt charged, as though the ground held secrets of untold power. In the distance, towering gates and monoliths stood sentinel, their surfaces etched with symbols that whispered of forgotten civilisations. The sun beat down from a cloudless sky, its rays harsh and unrelenting, casting long shadows over the jagged stones. The air was thin, making every breath a struggle.

Barbara heard the faint rustle of the wind as it moved through the ruins, carrying with it the distant echoes of voices — whispers of the past.

Gemma stood beside her, wiping dirt from her palms, her eyes wide. 'This is incredible, but we must look for the others.'

'Of course,' Barbara said. 'We'll have to search for them.'

Delf knelt, touching a stone block. 'These stones are thousands of years old. No one knows how they were carved so precisely. Some say it was the gods.'

As they stood in silence, absorbing the sheer majesty of the place, Barbara detected a strange pull — as if something was calling to her, drawing her deeper into the heart of the ruins. She looked around, scanning the horizon. In the distance, the jagged peaks of the Andes loomed, their snow-capped summits piercing the clouds.

But something wasn't right.

The air changed, growing colder despite the sun's heat.

A shadow passed over them. Barbara shivered, her instincts screaming that they were not alone.

A low, rhythmic chanting reached their ears, carried on the wind. It came from deeper within the ruins. Barbara exchanged a glance with Gemma and Delf, who had also heard it. Their faces mirrored her unease.

'We should move,' Delf said.

They followed the sound, stepping over the uneven ground, the sense of being watched growing stronger with each moment. The chanting grew louder, a strange, hypnotic melody. It was ancient, primal, a noise that resonated with the stones beneath their feet.

As they turned a corner, they were at the foot of a massive stone gate, its surface carved with intricate carvings of pumas, serpents, and figures locked in battle. Barbara's breath caught in her throat. She recognised the symbol — the Gate of the Puma, the legendary entrance to the heart of Pumapunku.

And standing before the gate were people draped in rough-spun cloth, their faces obscured by shadows. The chanting stopped as they approached, and one of the figures stepped forward. He was an old man, his face weathered and lined over time, his eyes sharp and bright.

'Welcome,' he said, his voice deep and commanding. 'You have come to where the world was born.'

Barbara's muscles tensed. There was something other-worldly about him, as if he existed simultaneously in the present and the distant past.

'Who are you?' Gemma asked.

He smiled, though it did not reach his eyes. 'I am the guardian of this place. We have been waiting for you.'

Delf stepped forward, his hand resting on the hilt of his dagger. 'Waiting for us?'

The old man looked at Barbara. 'Yes, the Valkyrie, the Elf and the scientist. The prophets foretold your visit. You are here because the end is near. The world is dying, and only you can prevent it.'

Gemma struggled to breathe, worried about her daughter and husband. 'What do you mean?'

'The Soulless are returning,' he said.

'How do we stop them?' Barbara asked.

The man's expression grew grave. 'There is a weapon, an ancient relic created by the Incas to defeat The Soulless. It is hidden deep within the sacred mountain, where no human has walked for centuries. If you do not retrieve it, The Soulless will rise, and the world as you know it will cease to exist.'

'Where is the weapon?' Delf said.

The old man gestured to the mountains beyond the ruins. 'It lies at the peak of Illimani, the sacred mountain of the Incas. But be warned, the journey is perilous. Many have tried to recover it and failed. The mountain is guarded by forces older than time itself.'

Gemma's throat tightened. 'Are my family here?'

He shook his head. 'Only you three.'

'How do we return to them?' Gemma asked.

'You need the Staff of Souls. Grip it and think of your destination; it will take you there when you complete your task.'

'We'll find the weapon,' Barbara said.

The old man nodded. 'You must hurry. The Soulless are stirring. The barrier to their realm is weakening; soon, they will break free. Come,' he added, turning to lead them through the Gate of the Puma. 'There is something you must see before you begin your journey.'

They followed him, the air growing colder and more

oppressive with each step. The chanting had ceased, leaving an eerie silence in its wake. The path led them deeper into the ruins, the walls closing around them, their surfaces etched with ancient symbols that pulsed with life. They emerged into a vast open chamber lined with statues of pumas, their eyes gleaming in the dim light. In the centre stood a massive stone altar, its surface covered in strange, glowing runes.

The old man gestured to the altar. 'This is the key. It will open the path to the sacred mountain but requires a sacrifice.'

Barbara's stomach twisted. 'What kind of sacrifice?'

The man's gaze shifted to her, his eyes dark and unreadable. 'Blood.'

Gemma gasped. 'You mean we have to—'

He nodded. 'A drop of blood shall suffice. But be warned, once the path is opened, there is no turning back.'

Barbara took a deep breath and pulled the dagger from her belt. She pressed the knife against her palm. A sharp pain shot through her as the blade broke the skin. She held her hand over the altar, letting the blood drip onto its surface.

For a moment, nothing happened. Then, the runes glowed brighter, their light filling the chamber with a soft, pulsating radiance. The air hummed with energy, and the ground trembled. The walls shifted, revealing a hidden passageway leading into the mountain's heart. A cold wind rushed out from the passage, carrying the scent of snow and ancient stone.

Barbara turned to Delf and Gemma. 'Are you ready?'

Gemma nodded, though her face was pale. Delf said nothing, his expression grim but resolute. Together, they stepped into the passage as the darkness swallowed them.

The path was treacherous, littered with small jagged rocks. The air grew colder with each step, and the walls closed around them. Barbara heard the distant rumble of the mountain as though it were alive, watching their every move.

The journey was long and gruelling, the cold biting at them, the thin air making each breath a struggle. As they neared the summit, the path became steeper, the ground slick with ice. Gemma's muscles screamed in protest, her body pushed to its limits. But she refused to stop, her mind focused on the weapon that lay ahead.

At last, they reached the peak.

The view from the top of the mountain was breathtaking, the world stretching out before them in a sea of snow and stone. But there was no time to admire the scenery.

They stood at the summit, breath ragged in the thin air, and gazed across the desolate expanse below. The Andes sprawled endlessly in every direction, a cold, indifferent wilderness of jagged peaks and plunging valleys, the sky a pale, featureless blue. The wind howled around them, biting at their exposed skin and carrying a deep sense of isolation. The world felt distant on the sacred mountain of Illimani, as if they had crossed into a place outside of time. But even in its stark beauty, something was unsettling.

They weren't alone.

Delf crouched at the edge of the plateau, studying the surroundings with the sharpness of a hunter. His muscles were taut, as though he, too, sensed the unseen things watching them from the shadows. Gemma stood closer to Barbara, her eyes filled with uncertainty.

'The air feels different here,' Gemma said. 'Like something is waiting.'

Barbara felt a tingling sensation at the base of her neck, an instinctive warning that danger was near. 'You're right.'

'Stay alert,' Delf muttered. 'This place is not as empty as it seems.'

Barbara stepped forward, her boots crunching on the frozen ground. Ahead of them, half-buried in snow and ice, stood an altar similar to the one they'd seen in Pumapunku but far more massive. Intricate patterns were carved into the stone, symbols of the Inca gods, and the unmistakable image of a puma locked in eternal combat with a shadowy figure. The weapon — their salvation — was hidden somewhere on this sacred site.

A low, rumbling noise echoed through the mountains as Barbara approached the altar. The ground trembled, and the stones shifted as if disturbed by something moving deep below.

'Did you hear that?' Gemma whispered.

Barbara knelt before the altar, brushing away the snow and ice that had accumulated over centuries. The stone was cold, almost painfully so, and as she cleared the surface, she saw that the runes were glowing, pulsing with a dim light that seemed to resonate with the energy of the mountain.

'This is colder than the land of the Frost Giants.'

'There's something powerful underneath it,' Delf said.

He reached for his dagger and began prying at the edges of the stone, searching for a way to lift the heavy slab. Barbara felt a rising sense of urgency. Whatever was beneath the altar was connected to their fate — but she could also feel the malevolent presence growing stronger, closing in around them.

The wind increased, howling like a beast. Barbara's hair whipped across her face, and the cold intensified, biting her skin. She glimpsed movement nearby — shadows flitting between the jagged rocks on the mountainside, too fast to be human.

'We're not alone,' she said. 'Something's watching us.'

Barbara stood, scanning the snow-covered landscape. The shadows were still there, moving closer, growing more distinct. She saw vague, humanoid shapes, but their movements were unnatural, jerky, as though they were not bound by the same physical rules as the living.

'Disciples of The Soulless,' Delf said, his hand tightening on his dagger.

Barbara reached into her jacket and removed another blade, handing it to Gemma. 'Use it if you have to.'

Gemma pointed at the moving shapes. 'They're coming for us.'

The shadows inched closer, their forms becoming more defined. They were tall and thin, their limbs elongated and distorted like giant spiders, their eyes glowing with an eerie, unnatural light. They moved silently, creeping over the snow without disturbing it as though they were part of the air around them.

'We need to move!' Delf shouted, his voice cutting through the rising panic.

Barbara grabbed the dagger she'd used earlier and slashed her palm again, letting the blood drip onto the altar. The runes glowed brighter, and the stone began to shift, grinding as it slid aside to reveal a dark opening beneath.

But the creatures were already upon them.

One of the beasts lunged at Gemma, its long, bony fingers reaching to grab her as she moved back. It hissed, its glowing eyes locking onto her, and it struck again, faster this time. Its nails clawed at her face as she thrust the dagger into its guts. It howled.

'Get down!' Delf bellowed, tackling the creature with

his full weight. The force of his attack knocked it off balance. It writhed and twisted, its limbs moving in ways that defied nature, before rising to its feet again, its glowing eyes fixed on him.

Barbara's blood dripped from her hand, her muscles tensing as her body screamed at her to defend her friends. She peered at the altar, the dark opening yawning before her like the mouth of a beast, waiting for something to happen. She'd travelled through numerous portals to know how they worked. It should have been shimmering by now.

Was it not enough blood? The wrong type of sacrifice?

An unknown force hit her in the hip, sending her tumbling into the pit and landing hard on the ground. Her eyes struggled to adjust to the darkness, but she sensed the weight of something ancient pressing down on her.

Deep in the shadows, she saw it: the weapon. Instead of a sword or spear, it was a staff crafted from dark wood and etched with gold. At the top was a puma's head, its eyes glowing with the same eerie light as the runes above. It hummed with power, and Barbara felt its energy pulsing in time with her heartbeat.

She reached for the staff, her fingers closing around its smooth surface. The moment she touched it, a jolt of electricity coursed through her, so powerful it nearly knocked her off her feet. It pulsed with life, its force filling her with strength and clarity. She saw the creatures above, their forms no longer shadowy but crystal clear.

Barbara scrambled out of the pit with the staff, her body vibrating with the weapon's power. The beasts had surrounded Delf and Gemma, their eyes glowing with hunger as they closed in for the kill.

'Stay back!' Barbara shouted, raising the staff.

A brilliant illumination exploded from the puma's eyes,

blinding in its intensity. The monsters screeched, their forms twisting and contorting as the light washed over them. The sound was unbearable, a high-pitched wail that reverberated through the mountains. One by one, the creatures disintegrated, their bodies turning to ash and blowing away on the wind.

The brightness faded, leaving the world in silence.

Barbara stood, her chest heaving, the staff still glowing in her hand. Delf and Gemma stared at her in awe, their faces pale.

'You did it,' Gemma said.

Barbara looked at the weapon. 'This is only the beginning.'

Gemma grinned. 'Now we can return to the others.'

All three of them gripped the staff and thought of the pyramid on the island.

Chapter 13

This Jungle

The island stretched out before them like a forgotten world, wild and untamed. Veronica and Catherine lingered at the edge of the dense jungle, where the beach's soft, white sand met the dark underbrush. They inhaled the scent of saltwater and the earthy trace of wet leaves. The calm but endless sea glistened in the late morning light while the forest seemed to hum with a life of its own - an ancient, hidden energy. For a moment, neither of them spoke. They stood there, soaking in the silence, the waves lapping at the shore.

It had been over a week since Catherine had woken from the coma that had swallowed her time and memories. Veronica could still barely believe her daughter was standing with her. Her heart swelled with joy and guilt. She'd missed so much and had been away for so long during Catherine's illness. Now, she was determined to make up for it. But even on the hidden island, their peaceful reunion was shadowed by the unspoken weight of Veronica's work—the Institute, the portals, the Elementals.

Veronica tasted the sharpness of the sea air and turned to Catherine. 'It feels different, doesn't it? This place.'

Catherine nodded, gazing across the horizon before she met her mother's gaze. 'It does, like it's alive. Like it's watching us.'

Veronica smiled. 'That's because it is. This island—it's more than just a place. It's connected in ways most people wouldn't understand.'

Catherine looked intrigued but said nothing. She had always been quiet and introspective. Since waking, she had been more so. Veronica saw it in her eyes—the questions she didn't know how to ask.

'We're not following the rest to the pyramid?' Catherine wondered.

Veronica shook her head. 'No, they'll be fine without us.' She peered into the greenery. 'But we should get some exercise and explore.'

They began walking opposite to where Ella and the others had gone earlier, crunching over fallen leaves and twigs as they ventured deeper into the jungle. The tall and ancient trees rose like towering sentinels, their branches entwined to form a canopy that filtered the sunlight into dappled patches on the ground. The air grew cooler as they moved farther from the beach, the scents shifting from salty ocean breezes to the rich, damp smells of the earth and greenery. The sounds of the wilderness surrounded them: birds calling, the rustling of leaves, the occasional crack of a branch underfoot. It was a world untouched by time, a place where nature ruled.

As they moved, Veronica glanced at Catherine now and then as if reassuring herself that her daughter was really with her. Catherine's face had lost the pallor it had taken on in the hospital, replaced by a healthy flush, though her movements were still careful, tentative as if she were adjusting to the world all over again.

Finally, Catherine broke the silence. 'You worked for the Institute. The people we're hiding from.'

Veronica felt her stomach tighten at the question. She'd known it would come, but hearing it aloud brought a rush of memories she wasn't sure she was ready to share. Yet, Catherine deserved the truth.

'Yes,' Veronica said, her voice steady but soft. 'I did. For years.'

'What did you do?' Catherine's tone wasn't accusatory, just curious. Still, it felt like a dagger of guilt twisting in Veronica's chest. How could she explain everything? The secret missions, the endless hours of research, the life she'd lived in shadows while her daughter had been left behind? And this was before the coma.

Veronica took a deep breath, trying to find the right words. 'I was part of a team that studies things. Things most people don't know exist. Portals, for one.' She paused, glancing at Catherine to gauge her reaction. Her daughter was listening, her expression unreadable.

'Portals?' Catherine repeated, the word foreign and strange on her tongue.

'Yes,' Veronica continued, 'portals between worlds, dimensions. They aren't just science fiction, Cat. They're real. And they're dangerous. The Institute—well, we searched for them. We tried to find them before they opened too wide and something that shouldn't crossed through.'

Catherine's brows furrowed. 'Something crosses through? Like what?'

Veronica's heart raced at the question. She remembered the first time she'd seen a portal open, the gaping maw in the fabric of reality, the strange, humming energy that had spilt through. And then... the creatures that had followed. Elementals, as they'd come to call them. Beings of pure force, born from the elements of their own worlds, wild and unpredictable.

'Elementals,' she said at last. 'They come from different realms. Each one is tied to an element—fire, water, earth, air. They stumble through these portals, often confused and disoriented. And when they do, it can be catastrophic.'

Catherine slowed her pace, processing everything. 'You're saying there are beings from other worlds? And they come here? Why doesn't anyone know about this?'

Veronica smiled. 'The Institute makes sure of that. We keep it quiet. Most people couldn't handle knowing what's out there. It's safer that way.'

'But *you* know?' Catherine's voice was softer now, almost hesitant.

Veronica nodded, her mind replaying her first encounter with an Elemental. It had been a Water Elemental, a swirling mass of liquid that had flowed through a portal in the middle of a small village. The destruction it caused had been overwhelming—floods that swallowed entire buildings, drowning fields and homes in minutes. She'd been part of the team that contained it, forced to watch as they trapped it in a containment field, its form thrashing and writhing as it was pulled back to its world.

'I've seen them,' she confirmed. 'And I've helped stop them. It's not something I expected to do with my life. But the work—well, it's important.'

Catherine was quiet again, her steps slow and measured as they continued through the jungle. After a few minutes, she spoke. 'Is that why you weren't there? When I was in the hospital?'

Veronica's heart sank. Here it was. The question she'd dreaded. She stopped walking, turning to face Catherine. The pain in her daughter's eyes was unmistakable, even though she tried to hide it.

'I'm sorry, Cat,' Veronica said, her voice thick with emotion. 'I believed I was doing the right thing. The Institute—something was happening, something urgent. I thought I had time before it got worse with you.'

Catherine shook her head, not in anger, but in sadness. 'I was in a coma, Mum. I didn't know anything. But when I woke up, and you weren't there...' Her voice trailed off.

Veronica stepped closer, reaching out to touch her daughter's arm. 'I'm here now. And I'm not going anywhere. I promise.'

They stood there, the sounds of the jungle filling the silence between them. Veronica felt the weight of her past decisions pressing down on her, the years she'd spent chasing portals and Elementals while missing out on Catherine's life. But she was determined to make things right, to rebuild the bond they'd lost.

Catherine touched the scar on her neck. 'It was Elementals that attacked us in Newcastle?'

Veronica nodded. 'Harpies.'

'And those with us here, they are also Elementals?'

'Some of them,' Veronica said. 'Seraphina, Barbara, Callisto, Kitty, Delf and Peg.' She thought it best not to tell her about the dragon and the centaur just yet. 'They're our friends.'

'They all came through portals into our world?'

'I don't know about Seraphina, but yes, the others.'

'And you worked with them at the Institute?'

'Sort of,' Veronica answered.

Catherine touched a leaf, surprised at its softness. 'It feels like we're in another world.'

Veronica smiled. 'You're right, it does.'

'You're not telling me everything though, are you, Mother?'

Veronica gripped her daughter's fingers. 'We have to take it slow, Cat. You're still recovering from the coma, and I don't want to put too much strain on you. I will tell you everything eventually, I promise.'

Catherine held her mother's hand. 'Some of it is bad, right?'

Pain and guilt swept through Veronica. 'Yes.'

Catherine pulled away from her. 'It's okay, Mum. I've done terrible things as well.'

Veronica was unsure if she should ask, changing the subject. 'You're feeling better now.'

Catherine nodded. 'I think Seraphina helped me.'

That surprised Veronica. 'Seraphina?'

'Yes,' Catherine replied. 'She was the one who brought me out of the coma, wasn't she?'

'Yes,' Veronica answered. 'She's a witch.'

Catherine laughed. 'That makes me remember those books you got for me as a kid - *The Worst Witch*. I loved those.'

'You loved reading. No wonder you went to university to study literature.'

They stood there for a while before Catherine spoke.

'Seraphina said she wanted to give me more of her Light, but she needed it to keep the island hidden. Were you studying Light at the Institute?'

'Not me, but the scientists were. They discovered

Elementals could cure ill people by transferring some of their Light into the sick.'

'What is Light?' Catherine asked.

Veronica shrugged. 'We don't know. It's energy, that's clear, but nothing the Institute had seen before. Ella knows more about it, but I haven't spoken to her about it since we arrived here.'

'She seems pretty important for a fourteen-year-old girl.'

Veronica nodded. 'She is.'

'But I sense some tension between you and her, Mum.'

Veronica smiled, happy the coma hadn't dulled Catherine's bright mind. 'I guess you could say that.'

Catherine studied her mother's face. 'Is this something to do with those bad things you mentioned?'

Veronica sighed. 'Unfortunately, yes.'

Catherine's stomach grumbled, and she laughed. 'We better continue this at the tent before I faint with hunger.'

Veronica pulled her daughter close. 'Well, we can't have that.'

They headed back in silence, but Veronica felt happier than she had in a long time.

Chapter 14

Eye of the Forgotten

Ella's stomach lurched as her surroundings twisted and dissolved, the familiar shapes of Stonehenge fading into a swirling mist. Lyssa's hand, cold and firm, gripped her fingers as they were pulled through a vortex of light and shadow. The ground disappeared beneath her, and for a moment, Ella felt weightless, like she was falling through an endless void. Her father's voice was lost in the rush of wind and brilliance, but she sensed his presence nearby, a steady anchor amid the chaos.

When the spinning stopped, Ella's feet slammed into solid ground with a jolt. She gasped, stumbling forward, but Lyssa caught her. Her father landed a moment later, arms flailing for balance.

'Where are we?' Andrew Finn muttered, straightening his jacket and squinting into their strange environment.

They stood on a barren plain under a stormy sky. The air was heavy, thick with moisture, as if a storm was moments away. The ground was uneven, scattered with sharp rocks and tall, wiry grass. A low mist clung to the ground, swirling around their ankles like spectral fingers. In the distance, jagged mountains loomed, their peaks shrouded in dark clouds that crackled with flashes of distant lightning. The wind carried the scent of damp earth and something acrid, like sulphur, which stung Ella's nostrils and made her eyes water.

'This is the Realm of The Soulless,' Lyssa said. 'We are far from the world you know, but you must retrieve what was hidden here. It is the only way for you to return home.'

Ella's heart pounded as she surveyed their surroundings. The place felt wrong. The oppressive air pressed on her chest, making breathing difficult. It was as though the essence of life had been drained from the land, leaving behind only a hollow shell of what once was.

'Who are you?' Ella said.

Lyssa gazed at her. 'I was a prisoner of The Soulless. I escaped but ended up here a long time ago. I know some of their secrets.'

'What are we looking for?' Andrew asked, glancing warily at Lyssa. His voice sounded distant, swallowed up by the vast, empty expanse.

Lyssa turned to face them, her blue eyes glinting. 'You seek the Eye of the Forgotten. An ancient artefact created by The Soulless long ago. It is the key to understanding their power and defeating them.'

'And to getting us home?' Ella asked.

Lyssa nodded. 'Yes.'

Ella frowned. 'Why would something so important be here?'

'The Soulless once ruled this realm,' Lyssa explained, her gaze drifting toward the distant mountains. 'It was their sanctuary, a place of exile after they were cast out from the realms of the living. They left many scattered and hidden creations behind to prevent anyone from undoing their work. The Eye is one such creation. You must find it before it falls into the wrong hands.'

Andrew rubbed his chin, deep in thought. 'And what does this Eye do?'

Lyssa hesitated, her expression darkening. 'It allows you to see into the hearts of humans, to strip away their souls, leaving only emptiness behind. In the claws of The Soulless, it was a weapon of unimaginable power.'

Ella shivered. 'And if we don't find it?'

Lyssa's gaze locked onto Ella's, her voice grave. 'If The Soulless regain the Eye, they will use it to sever the bond between Light and life. The consequences would be... catastrophic.'

Ella touched her chest. 'You know about Light?'

Lyssa glanced above them. 'Yes, but not that which illuminates the heavens.' She pointed at Ella. 'It lives inside you.' Then she looked at Andrew. 'Your Light vanished long ago, disappearing as you aged. Do you miss it?'

He shook his head. 'You can't miss what you never knew you had.'

Lyssa laughed. 'You're wrong.'

'How can this Eye get us home?' Ella said.

'One touch of the artefact will return you to the one that sent you here,' Lyssa replied.

Andrew exchanged a worried glance with Ella. 'Okay. Let's find this thing.'

Lyssa turned and led them across the barren landscape. Ella and her father followed, the wind tugging at their clothes as they walked. The terrain was rough, littered with sharp stones and deep crevices that forced them to navigate carefully. The mist thickened as they went, wrapping around them like a veil, making it difficult to see more than a few feet ahead.

With each step, the oppressive silence weighed on Ella. There was no birdsong, no rustling of leaves or chirping insects—just the soft crunch of their footsteps on the rocky ground and the distant rumble of thunder. The absence of life made the land feel desolate and abandoned.

'This place gives me the creeps,' Andrew muttered, kicking a loose rock aside. 'Feels like we're walking through a graveyard.'

Ella nodded, scanning the horizon. 'Yeah. It's too quiet.'

Her father gasped. 'Look at that.'

She followed his gaze, seeing how the barren landscape had changed to a verdant, green terrain. But it wasn't that holding her father's attention – dozens of large emerald rocks floated in the air. Some were only a few feet off the ground, while others touched the clouds.

Ella had witnessed many strange things in the last few years, but this held her breath. 'How is that possible?'

'You must forget all thoughts about what is possible and not here,' Lyssa said. 'The Realm of The Soulless defies all known human understanding.'

'Right,' Ella replied as she approached the closest floating rock.

'Be careful,' Andrew Finn cautioned.

She acknowledged his warning but reached for the stone, touching the damp moss covering it. It felt like the wet grass she knew from home. She clambered up with a sense of adventure, hoping to get a better view of their surroundings.

Her father moved to her side. 'Are you okay, Ella?'

She nodded. 'There's a lot of green ahead of us and more of these hovering stones.' She stood briefly, a cool breeze wrapping around her, before getting down. 'What now?'

'We keep moving,' Lyssa answered.

Ella watched the other girl go on as her father grabbed her hand and lowered his voice. 'Let's not take any risks.'

Lyssa, walking several steps in front, turned to face them. 'We are not alone.'

Ella froze. 'What do you mean?'

'There are watchers here,' Lyssa said. 'They will not interfere, but they are always watching.'

Andrew frowned. 'Great. Just what we needed.'

As they continued, Ella sensed a presence lurking beyond her vision. It felt like a thousand unseen eyes scrutinising their every move, hidden in the swirling haze and the floating rocks. Her skin prickled with unease, and she couldn't shake the feeling that something—or someone— was following them.

They approached a large stone structure, its jagged edges jutting out of the ground like the ribs of a long-dead creature. The mist swirled around the stones as if drawn to them, and a faint, pulsating glow emanated from inside the formation.

'This is it,' Lyssa said, stopping at the base of the rocks. 'The Eye is hidden within. You must retrieve it.'

Ella stepped forward, taking a deep breath. The light pulsed like a heartbeat, drawing her closer. She sensed a strange energy radiating from the stones, a cold, tingling sensation that made her skin crawl.

'How do we get inside?' Andrew asked, eyeing the rocks.

Lyssa gestured toward a narrow opening between two of the stones. 'The way is open. But be warned: The Soulless left guardians to protect the Eye. They will not allow you to take it without a fight.'

'Guardians?' Ella's voice wavered. 'What guardians?'

'Automata,' Lyssa said. 'Ancient machines designed to defend the relic at all costs. They have no souls, no emotions. They cannot be reasoned with.' She sighed. 'Several times, I have just escaped their clutches.'

Andrew let out a low whistle. 'This just keeps getting better.'

Ella swallowed hard, steeling herself. 'We've come this far. We can't turn back now.'

She ducked into the narrow opening, her father and Lyssa following behind. The passage was dark and cramped, the air cold and musty. The walls were smooth, and the faint glow from within provided enough illumination to guide them.

The strange pulsing light grew stronger as they ventured deeper into the rock formation, casting eerie shadows everywhere. The tunnel twisted and turned, descending like a spiral staircase into the earth. Ella's breath came in short, shallow gasps, the air thick with the scent of damp stone and something metallic, like rusted iron. They emerged into a vast chamber, the high ceiling swallowed by the gloom above. A pedestal stood in the centre, and the Eye of the Forgotten rested atop it.

The artefact was unlike anything Ella had ever seen, a smooth, spherical object, about the size of a fist, made of a dark, glassy material that shimmered with an inner glow. Strange, intricate symbols were etched into its surface, glowing in the gloom. As she stared at it, Ella felt an overwhelming dread, as if the air around the Eye was charged with malice.

Andrew took a cautious step forward, gazing at the artefact. 'That's it, isn't it?'

Before Ella could respond, a low, grinding sound echoed through the chamber. She spun in time to see the walls shift and open, revealing tall, humanoid figures made of metal. Their eyes glowed with an eerie red light, and their limbs moved with a mechanical precision that made her shiver.

'The guardians,' Lyssa whispered. 'They have awakened.'

The automata stepped forward, their movements fluid and lifelike. Ella's heart raced as they closed in, their metal bodies gleaming in the gloom. Each was armed with long, jagged blades attached to their arms.

Andrew pulled Ella behind him. 'What do we do?'

'There's no fighting them,' Lyssa said, her voice urgent. 'You must get to the Eye. Once it's in your possession, they will no longer be a threat.'

Ella's mind raced. The automata were closing in, their footsteps echoing in the chamber. She felt the weight of the situation pressing down on her, knowing that failure meant more than just their lives—it signified The Soulless regaining their power.

And it meant not returning home to her friends – to her mother.

Determination surged through her. Ella darted toward the pedestal. The automata reacted, their glowing eyes locking onto her as they moved to intercept. But she was faster, her legs pumping with adrenaline as she reached out and grabbed the Eye of the Forgotten.

When her fingers closed around the artefact, a blinding radiance erupted from its surface, flooding the chamber with a brilliant, golden glow. The automata froze; their red eyes dimmed as the light washed over them. The air hummed with energy, and Ella felt the power of the Eye beating beneath her fingertips.

For a brief, breathless moment, the world seemed to stand still.

Then, as suddenly as it had begun, the glow faded, leaving the chamber in darkness. The automata remained motionless, their lifeless forms frozen like statues in ice.

Ella exhaled, clutching the Eye. 'We did it.'

Andrew let out a relieved laugh. 'You did it, kid.'

Lyssa stepped forward, her expression unreadable. 'You have the Eye. But the journey is far from over. Now, you must learn to use it.'

Ella stared at the artefact, its smooth surface cool against her skin. She sensed its power, ancient and dangerous, like a pulse beneath her fingertips.

'You said it would transport us home when I touched it.'

'It will, once you connect it to the Book of All Life.'

Ella stepped back. 'You know about the Book?'

Lyssa nodded. 'I sense it in your bag.'

Ella didn't like this, but what choice did she have? 'How?'

Lyssa's blue eyes glinted in the gloom. 'You must learn to wield its power before The Soulless find you. Only then can you hope to stop them.'

'Yeah, great, but that doesn't answer my question. How do I connect the Eye of the Forgotten to the Book of All Life?'

'How does the Book work?' Lyssa asked.

Ella hesitated. Was this all a ploy to trick her into explaining the secrets of the Book of All Life? Why should she trust this stranger?

'Who are you really?' Ella said.

'I told you,' Lyssa replied.

Ella inched closer to her father. 'I don't believe you.'

Lyssa shrugged. 'Then we are all stuck here forever.'

The silence hung heavy before them before Andrew Finn spoke.

'We'll have to trust her, Ella.'

Ella knew she had no choice. She sat with the Eye of the Forgotten between her legs. Then she removed the Book of All Life from her bag and opened it.

'All I have to do is touch a blank part of a page and think of an Elemental, and it will appear.'

'So,' her father said. 'If you do that and imagine a unicorn, it will come here?'

She laughed. 'Yeah, I've already done that.'

'Wow!' he replied. 'But how will that get us home?'

They both looked at Lyssa.

'Touch the page, but don't think of an Elemental. Picture the Eye of the Forgotten, and it will appear in the book.'

'And then?' Ella asked.

'Then,' Lyssa answered. 'You picture in your mind the Eye of the Forgotten taking you where you want to go.'

Ella doubted what she was hearing, but she had no choice.

She placed a finger on the page, and an image of the Eye of the Forgotten shimmered into place inside the Book of All Life. Ella removed her finger and looked at her father.

Then she touched the image again.

Chapter 15

The Warden of Souls

Seraphina calmed her mind with an incantation learned centuries ago. She glanced at Callisto, whose eyes locked on the Guardian, her muscles coiled with tension. The air crackled with energy, and the setting sun bathed the desert in deep amber and blood-red hues.

'Choose,' the Guardian repeated, his voice softer but more ominous, like the whisper of a storm approaching the horizon. 'The Warden of Souls does not wait. You are the one to fulfil the prophecy or will be consumed by it.'

Seraphina stared at him. 'Why me? I didn't ask for this. I didn't seek the Warden of Souls.'

The Guardian's smile faded. 'It is not a matter of asking. The Warden's return is part of the natural order woven into the fabric of time. You were chosen because of your lineage, witch. You and your companions are bound to this fate, whether or not you wish it.'

A cold gust of wind swept the desert, stirring the sand around their feet. The sound of the marketplace had faded, leaving them in an eerie stillness beneath the shadow of the

Sphinx. Seraphina sensed Callisto tensing beside her, her massive form vibrating with anticipation. The bear, too, understood the gravity of the situation.

'Tell us what we should do,' Callisto growled, her deep voice cutting through the silence like a blade.

The Guardian's eyes flicked to Callisto, then back to Seraphina. 'The Warden of Souls resides in the realm between life and death. You must journey there to retrieve an artefact that will awaken or bind him forever.'

Seraphina shivered. Travel to the realm between life and death? That kind of magic was beyond anything she'd encountered. 'And how are we supposed to reach this place?'

The Guardian lifted his hand, and the sand at his feet swelled and shifted. An object emerged from the ground—a small stone amulet etched with runes that glowed in the fading light. He offered it to Seraphina. 'This shall serve as your guide. It is linked to the artefact and will show you the way.'

Seraphina hesitated before stepping forward and taking the talisman from him. The moment her fingers closed around it, a sharp jolt of energy shot through her, and for a brief second, her vision blurred. She saw flashes of a dark, twisted landscape where the sky was an endless black void, and bones littered the ground—the realm between life and death.

She gasped, stumbling back as the sight faded.

Callisto moved closer, her fur bristling. 'Are you all right?'

Seraphina nodded, though her heart still raced. 'I saw it. The realm. It's not a place for the living.'

The Guardian lowered his hand, the sand settling once more. 'No, it is not. But the amulet can protect you for a time. However, you must be swift. The longer you stay there, the more difficult it will be to return.'

Seraphina closed her eyes, steadying herself. There was no other way. She had to do it. 'How do we get there?'

The Guardian's expression darkened. 'Follow the amulet's pull. It will take you to the gateway—a portal deep beneath the Great Pyramid. But beware, the path is protected.'

'By what?' Callisto asked.

The Guardian smiled again, but there was no warmth this time. 'By the creatures that dwell in the shadows between worlds. They will sense your presence when you enter their domain and will not hesitate to drag you into the abyss.'

Seraphina's grip tightened on the amulet. She had no idea what these shadow creatures were, but she'd faced worse. She had to believe that for Ella and the others.

'We'll handle it,' she said. 'Thank you for your help.'

The Guardian's smile faded, and he turned away without another word, his soldiers following. As they disappeared into the desert, Seraphina wondered what waited for them in the realm between life and death.

'Well,' Callisto muttered, glancing at the pyramids in the distance, 'we'd better get moving.'

Seraphina nodded. The amulet pulsed, a faint tug pulling her toward the Great Pyramid. She recognised magic within it, ancient and powerful, guiding her steps. The sky had turned a deep indigo, the first stars twinkling in the fading light as they strode across the desert. The wind picked up, swirling the sand around them in whispers. As they walked, the barren landscape seemed to stretch in every direction, the pyramids looming larger as they approached.

Seraphina's thoughts raced as she followed the pull of the amulet. The Warden of Souls. The prophecy. It all felt too big, too overwhelming. She wasn't a hero. She was just a witch trying to protect the people she cared about.

'Stop overthinking,' Callisto said, her voice stern but not unkind. 'We've dealt with worse. We'll deal with this.'

Seraphina smiled though her nerves gnawed at her. 'You're right. One step at a time.'

The entrance to the Great Pyramid was a gaping maw of darkness, hidden among the crumbling stone at the base. The closer they got, the more Seraphina detected the magic pulsing beneath the surface, like a heartbeat buried deep within the earth.

Callisto touched the old stone. 'How do we get inside?'

The amulet pulsed in Seraphina's hand, drawing her closer to the entrance. She pushed it against the stone, and a doorway slithered open. They stepped inside, the cool air of the pyramid contrasting the desert heat. The walls were smooth and cold to the touch, and the faint glow of the amulet illuminated the narrow passage ahead.

The tunnel twisted and turned, descending deeper, the atmosphere growing heavier with each step. The silence was suffocating, broken only by their footsteps echoing off the walls. A thin mist clung to their faces like a spider's web.

Seraphina sensed they were being watched as they ventured further. Shadows flickered at the edges of her vision, but when she turned to look, there was nothing there.

'We're close,' she whispered.

Callisto grunted in acknowledgement. The passage opened into a vast chamber, the high ceiling disappearing into darkness. In the centre of the room stood a massive stone altar, and beyond it, a swirling vortex of dark energy—a portal, just as the Guardian had said.

But they weren't alone.

Figures emerged from the gloom, their forms twisted and grotesque - shadow creatures. Their eyes glowed with an unnatural light, and their movements were jerky and disjointed as if they didn't belong in this world.

Callisto growled, stepping forward to place herself between Seraphina and the monsters. 'Looks like we've got company.'

Seraphina held up the amulet, letting its magic surge through her. The creatures hesitated, their glowing eyes fixed on the stone in her hand.

'We have to reach the portal,' Seraphina said. 'It's the only way.'

The monsters hissed, their bodies shifting and rippling like smoke. One lunged toward them, its claws outstretched. Callisto roared, swiping at the beast with her massive paw. It shrieked as it dissolved into shadow, but more were already closing in.

'Go!' Callisto shouted, her voice echoing through the chamber. 'I'll hold them off!'

Seraphina hesitated for a split second, her heart clenching at the thought of leaving Callisto to face the creatures alone. But there was no time to argue. She had to trust that the bear could handle herself.

Clutching the amulet, she dodged the things that swarmed around her. The portal crackled with dark energy, its pull growing stronger the closer she got. She felt the weight of the realm beyond it, a place where time and reality bent and twisted.

Seraphina sprinted to the altar. She turned to see Callisto still fighting, her powerful limbs keeping the creatures at bay. But they were relentless, and more poured from the shadows with every passing second.

'Callisto!' Seraphina shouted, her voice raw with urgency. 'We have to go, now!'

Callisto glanced back at her, then with a roar that shook the chamber, she barrelled through the remaining monsters and ran toward the portal.

Seraphina didn't wait. She raised the amulet, and the portal flared with blinding light. Taking a deep breath, she stepped forward—and everything went black.

The world shifted around her, the sensation of falling and spinning all at once. For a moment, Seraphina thought she was lost in the void, suspended between life and death. But then the darkness receded, and she stood on solid earth.

She blinked, her vision adjusting to the gloom. The realm between life and death was even more terrifying than she'd imagined. The sky was a swirling mass of black clouds, the air thick with the stench of decay. The ground was cold and hard, littered with bones and the flesh of the dead. A pile of decapitated heads lay nearby. Some seemed to be alive, blinking at her.

Callisto appeared beside her. 'This place reeks.'

Seraphina nodded, studying the desolate landscape. The amulet glowed in her hand, guiding her toward their destination. 'Let's find this artefact and get out of here.'

They moved through the realm, every sound amplified in the eerie silence. The wind howled, and shadows flickered at the edges of their vision. It felt like they were being watched, though there was no sign of living—or dead—beings.

The amulet's pull grew stronger as they neared a massive stone structure in the distance. It was a temple, ancient and crumbling, its walls covered in strange symbols and runes. The artefact had to be inside.

They approached the entrance, but as they stepped through the threshold, a sudden wave of cold washed over them. Seraphina shivered, her breath visible in the frigid air. At the centre was a pedestal, and a small, carved stone orb rested on it.

Seraphina reached for it, but the ground trembled before her fingers could touch the surface. The walls groaned, and from the shadows emerged a figure—a being of pure darkness, its eyes glowing with an eerie light.

'The Warden of Souls,' Seraphina whispered.

The Warden stepped forward. Its form was a mass of swirling flesh, with multiple arms and legs extending from its large torso. It moved on three legs, limbs thick as tree trunks with strange insects clinging to them.

Its voice echoed in the chamber like a thousand whispers. 'You seek the artefact, but do you know the price?'

Seraphina swallowed hard, focused on the Warden. 'I'm here to fulfil the prophecy. I'll do whatever it takes.'

The Warden's eyes glowed brighter, and it extended a hand toward her: it had ten fingers that wriggled like worms. 'Then you must choose. Awaken me... or bind me forever. The choice is yours, and once made, it cannot be undone.'

'Why would we waken you?' Callisto said.

The Warden laughed, releasing little spiders from its mouth that fell to the ground and skittered into the shadows. 'Because I am the only thing that can control The Soulless.'

'How would you do that?' Seraphina asked.

It inched towards her, evil seeping out of it in tiny black wisps. One touched her hand, and pain swept through Seraphina. She struggled to concentrate but dragged the Light she wasn't using to protect the island up from the depths of her soul to force the darkness off her.

'Every living creature must die,' the Warden said. 'Even The Soulless. And I am the Lord of the Dead.' Its eyes shimmered through yellow, red and black. 'But I must be in the living world to stop them.'

'Then you'll return here?' Seraphina asked.

'Perhaps,' the Warden replied.

One evil to defeat another?

Seraphina hesitated, considering her choices. Awaken the Warden and risk unleashing unimaginable power upon the world? Or bind it and hope they could stop The Soulless without it?

Her head ached, but there was no time for doubt. She had to choose.

She pointed at the orb. 'What is that?'

The Warden crept closer towards her. 'That is my heart.'

With a deep breath, Seraphina reached for the artefact, her fingers closing around the smooth, cold stone. The Warden watched her, silent and still, as she decided.

The moment she touched it, the temple shook. A blinding light erupted from the pedestal, and Seraphina detected the power of the Warden surging through her.

'Seraphina!' Callisto shouted, but her voice was lost in the roar.

Seraphina clenched her jaw, focusing all her will on her decision. She channelled the magic into the artefact, binding the Warden's power to it, sealing the creature away.

The light faded, and the temple fell silent.

Seraphina staggered back, the weight of the magic

nearly overwhelming her. But she had done it. The Warden of Souls was bound, its power contained.

Callisto rushed to her side, her eyes wide with concern. 'Are you okay?'

Seraphina nodded, her body trembling from the strain. 'I did it. The Warden is stuck there.'

The air around them began to shift and dissolve, the artefact's magic pulling them away. With a final, blinding flash of light, they left the realm between life and death and the portal closed behind them. Seraphina collapsed, exhausted but relieved.

Callisto helped her up. 'Is that it? Are we back?'

Seraphina stood, studying the walls. 'It looks like the pyramid but a different room from where we were with the others.'

'Let's find them,' Callisto said.

Seraphina followed her, the orb vibrating in her hand.

And whispers in her head.

Chapter 16

The Necronomicon

Kitty Stardust stared at Dr Dee, his yellowed teeth gleaming in the gloom. The fire in the hearth crackled. Kitty's mind hummed with Dee's words — Aleister Crowley. She'd heard that name whispered in darkened alleyways and inscribed in forbidden texts during her imprisonment at the Institute, where secrets and horrors intertwined.

She felt her pulse quickening, a steady beat in her ears. 'Steal it from Crowley?'

Dr Dee gave a slow, deliberate nod, his eyes gleaming with a strange mixture of amusement and malevolence. 'Indeed. The Book of the Dead resides with him now. If you wish to return home, you'll need it.'

The warmth of the fire did nothing to ease the icy knot of anxiety tightening in Kitty's gut. The air in the room felt oppressive.

Peg's green eyes shimmered. 'If it's a heist you're after, we've got no choice, do we?'

Kitty took a deep breath, the scent of dust and ancient parchment invading her senses as she studied the room.

The strange figurines lining the shelves seemed to leer at her, their faces glowing in the flickering firelight. Relics of power filled the place, but none of it felt safe. A sense of danger lurked in the air, a hidden threat waiting to reveal itself.

'Where can we find Crowley?' Kitty asked.

Dr Dee shifted beneath the layers of blankets, his eyes narrowing as if calculating their worth. His long, bony fingers tapped against the bedpost as he considered his answer.

'He frequents a certain gentleman's club,' Dee said. 'One not so easily found by the common folk. You'll need to head to the East End, near the docks. There, in a place called The Serpent's Coil, you'll find him. But be careful — Crowley surrounds himself with those who dabble in dark arts far beyond your understanding.'

Kitty shivered. She glanced at Peg, who pulled her hood over her long green hair.

'Then we should leave now,' Peg said, turning toward the door.

Kitty hesitated, feeling Lulu's presence prickling at the edges of her mind. The voice was quiet for once, but the weight of its watchful gaze remained. She knew Lulu was waiting to see how she would handle the situation and if fear would get the better of her.

You're not scared, are you? Lulu asked.

Kitty ignored her.

'Thank you,' she muttered to Dr Dee, though gratitude was the last thing she felt. She followed Peg out of the room, the door creaking shut behind them.

As they entered the cold London night, the stench of soot, damp stone, and burning wood filled Kitty's lungs. The sky was dark, a blanket of smoke obscuring the stars.

The narrow cobblestone streets were slick with rainwater, reflecting the dull glow of gas lamps. The distant sound of carriage wheels rattling against the stones echoed faintly, mingling with the occasional shout from a nearby alleyway.

Kitty pulled her shawl tighter around her, her ears twitching at every noise. She heard the murmur of voices in the shadows and the rustle of fabric as unseen figures moved through the fog. This part of London felt alive with secrets, a living entity filled with dark corners and hidden dangers.

The East End was even worse than she remembered.

'I don't like this place,' she muttered, keeping her voice low as they moved deeper into the maze of streets.

Peg glanced at her, scanning their surroundings with sharp awareness. 'Neither do I. But we've got no choice. Keep your head down, and try not to draw attention.'

Easier said than done, Kitty thought. Being a six-foot-tall cat was the very definition of attention-grabbing.

As they moved closer to the docks, the smell of saltwater and decaying fish overpowered the smoke and grime. The buildings were lofty and narrow, their crooked windows staring down at them like the hollow eyes of the dead. The sounds of the river lapping against the piers mixed with the low hum of conversation drifting from the taverns lining the streets.

The Serpent's Coil wasn't hard to find. The establishment sat between two warehouses, its entrance marked by a sign depicting a coiled serpent, its fanged mouth open in a silent hiss. The air around it seemed different, heavier, like stepping into somewhere the world's natural laws didn't apply.

Kitty hesitated as they reached the door, her heart howling. There was something about the place that set her on edge, an unseen force that made her fur prickle.

Peg noticed her hesitation and gave her a reassuring nod. 'We'll be in and out. Just keep your wits about you.'

Kitty took a deep breath, the scent of damp wood and iron filling her lungs, and pushed the door open. Shadows filled the tavern's interior, the thick smell of pipe smoke and alcohol mixing with the tang of something metallic and sour. The floorboards creaked as they stepped inside, the sound drawing a few curious glances from the scattered patrons. It was a strange crowd, a mix of finely dressed gentlemen in waistcoats and top hats mingling with those who looked far less respectable. Kitty sensed something off about them, an undercurrent of power humming below the surface. She glimpsed outlandish tattoos peeking out from beneath cuffs and collars, symbols she recognised from the occult texts she'd once been forced to study.

Lulu stirred in the back of her mind, her voice a low murmur. *They're not like the others. These people are dangerous, Kitty. Keep your claws ready.*

Kitty followed Peg toward the bar, studying the room. She spotted a group huddled in a corner, deep in conversation. One wore a dark suit, his head bowed as he spoke. A faint glint of gold caught Kitty's eye — the man was holding a small, ornate book.

The *Necronomicon*.

'That's him,' Peg whispered, nodding toward the man. 'Crowley.'

Kitty's breath stopped in her throat. This was their chance.

But as they approached him, a figure stepped from the shadows, blocking their path. The bloke was tall and thin, his face pale and gaunt. His eyes gleamed with malice as he looked them up and down, a sneer curling his lips.

'Where do you think you're going?'

Kitty tensed, her claws itching to extend. She could smell the danger rolling off him in waves, a sour stench that made her stomach churn.

'We're just passing through,' Peg said, her voice calm. 'No need for trouble.'

The man's sneer widened. 'Passing through, are you? To see Crowley, I'd wager.' He glanced over at the corner where Crowley sat, his eyes narrowing. 'He doesn't take kindly to uninvited guests.'

Kitty felt the weight of the room pressing in on them, the other patrons studying them. 'We're not here to cause problems. We must speak with him. It's important.'

The man's gaze flicked to Kitty, lingering on her feline features that didn't appear to bother him. His sneer deepened, and she saw the knife tucked into his belt.

'Important, is it?' he said. 'Well, I'm afraid you'll have to get in line.'

Before Kitty could react, Peg stepped forward, her eyes flashing with determination. 'Move aside. We don't have time for this.'

The man hesitated, his eyes narrowing as he sized her up. Then, a thin mist drifted out of Peg's open mouth. The bloke gasped, too slow to move, as the vapour shot forward between his trembling lips. His hands jerked to his throat as his legs buckled, clutching at his neck as he choked. Peg watched him for a second. Then she waved a hand, and an emerald haze crept out of his nose.

They stepped over him, but the tension in the air didn't dissipate. Every step felt like walking on a knife's edge, the atmosphere engulfing them as they approached Crowley's table. Crowley didn't look up from the book when they reached him. His fingers traced the intricate symbols etched into the cover, his lips moving in a silent chant.

Kitty exchanged a glance with Peg before clearing her throat. 'Crowley?'

He looked up, his dark eyes locking onto Kitty's with a sharp intensity that made her fur stand on end. Something was unsettling about his gaze, making her feel like he could see right through her. He said nothing, his gaze flicking between Kitty and Peg. Then, he closed the book and set it on the table before him.

'Well, my dear, which realm spawned you?'

'I was born in England,' Kitty replied.

He laughed. 'I want to visit that version of Albion.'

Peg moved closer. 'We require your help, Master Crowley.'

He turned to her. 'I know why you're here. But the *Necronomicon* isn't for you.'

Kitty's heart sank. She hadn't expected it to be easy, but the ice in his tone made her stomach twist with dread.

'We need it to return home,' Kitty said, trying to keep the desperation out of her voice. 'It's the only way.'

Crowley leaned back in his chair, his fingers lingering beneath his chin as he regarded them with a calculating gaze. For a moment, the room was silent, the only sound the distant murmur of voices and the crackling of the fire in the hearth.

Then, a smile crept across his face. 'I'll give you the book,' he said, his voice dripping with malice. 'But only if you're willing to pay the price.'

Kitty's blood ran cold. She didn't need to ask what he meant. The glint in his eyes told her everything she needed to know.

There's always a price, Lulu whispered, her voice filled with dark amusement.

Kitty's heart raced as she looked at Peg, who met her

gaze with a grim expression. They both knew it wouldn't be good whatever Crowley was asking for.

But they had no choice.

'What's the price?' Kitty asked.

Crowley's smile widened, his eyes gleaming with a cruel satisfaction.

'I want a soul,' he said. 'Yours, or hers.'

Kitty's breath caught in her throat. The room closed around her, the air thick with tension and the faint smell of sulphur.

Time seemed to stand still.

Kitty's pulse hammered in her ears. Her claws flexed, the tips grazing the worn wooden table before her. Across from her, Crowley's cruel smile deepened as though savouring her hesitation. Peg stood rigid beside her, the glow of the hearth casting sharp shadows over her angular features.

'A soul?' Her voice was low but firm. 'That's the price?'

He didn't blink, his fingers drumming on the cover of the *Necronomicon*. The silence in the room imprisoned them, broken only by the soft crackle of the fire and the murmurs of the tavern's other patrons.

'Indeed,' Crowley added, his voice smooth and unhurried. 'I have no interest in your trinkets, your gold, or whatever pathetic currencies you might offer. I deal in more lasting exchanges. And I require a soul — fresh, untainted.'

Kitty ignored Lulu's shouts for her to flee. Peg's hand twitched beside her though she said nothing. The weight of what Crowley demanded hung between them like a noose. She opened her mouth to protest, to refuse, but the faint brush of Peg's fingers on her arm stopped her. She turned to face her friend, meeting Peg's steady gaze. There was something unspoken in her eyes, a determination that made Kitty's chest tighten.

'Don't,' Kitty whispered, her throat dry. 'We'll find another way.'

Peg shook her head, a small, grim smile on her lips. 'There isn't another way, Kitty. This is it.'

'No,' Kitty insisted, her voice rising. 'Not like this.'

Crowley's soft laughter cut through the tension like a blade. 'A touching display of friendship. But I'm afraid sentiment won't save you here. A soul or nothing.'

The words echoed in Kitty's mind. Her gaze darted to the *Necronomicon*, its ornate cover gleaming in the firelight. Everything they needed to return home was within reach — and yet impossibly far. She sensed Lulu's presence coiling in her mind, watching, waiting.

There's always another way, Lulu hissed. *We need to leave.*

'I'll do it,' Peg said.

Kitty turned to her in horror. 'No! Peg, you can't—'

'I can,' Peg interrupted. 'And I will. You're not losing your soul for this, Kitty. I won't let you.'

Before Kitty could protest further, Peg stood before Crowley. Her green eyes shimmered with something fierce and determined.

Crowley's smile widened as he leaned forward, resting his elbows on the table. 'Ah, the selfless act of a true friend. How noble. Your soul will taste even sweeter for that.'

Kitty's chest tightened as she watched Peg. She knew there was no talking her out of this. Peg was stubborn and brave - too brave for her own good.

'No,' Kitty repeated, more to herself than anyone else. Desperation surged through her, searching for a solution, for some way to escape this nightmare.

Peg turned to Kitty, her expression softening for just a moment. 'You're going to get home, Kitty. I promise.'

Kitty opened her mouth to respond, but the words died in her throat as Crowley stood, his shadowy figure looming over them.

'A creature without a soul is a terrible thing,' he said. 'Especially a thinking one. You'll endure an eternity of pain and suffering. Do you understand that?'

Peg nodded. 'Yes.'

'Very well,' he said, his voice a low purr. 'The soul is yours to give?'

'Yes.'

Kitty's fur bristled as he moved closer, his presence oppressive and dark. She sensed his power in the air, and coldness seeped into her bones. The tavern seemed to fade away, the walls receding into darkness as he raised his hand. His fingers were long and thin, and the air trembled when he spoke.

'I will take what is owed.'

Peg stood tall, unflinching, as Crowley reached toward her. Kitty watched in horror, her muscles tense and ready to pounce, knowing that any movement would be futile.

As Crowley's hand neared Peg, a blinding illumination erupted from the space between them. The force of it sent Kitty stumbling backwards, and her eyes squeezed shut against the brightness. A deafening sound, like the roar of a hurricane, filled the air, drowning out all other noise. The bright glowing radiance hovered over Crowley, and Kitty heard something whispering to him – threatening the mage, whose face turned ashen.

Then, just as quickly as it began, the light vanished.

Kitty blinked; her eyesight blurred as she tried to understand what had happened. The room was still, the eerie silence pressing in around her. She heard her breathing, shallow and ragged. Her chest ached. When her vision cleared, she saw Crowley, but something was different. His expression, once so smug and cold, was twisted in confusion and fury. His outstretched hand trembled, and a dark shadow flickered across his face.

However, Peg remained untouched, standing tall with a fierce glow from within her. Her entire body shimmered with a strange, mystical glow — something ancient and ethereal.

'What... what is this?' Crowley whispered.

Peg's eyes blazed as she looked at him, her voice calm but decisive. 'You won't be taking my soul tonight. My Light doesn't belong to the likes of you.'

He recoiled, his expression darkening. 'You tricked me,' he snarled, his voice venomous. 'You wretched creature—'

Peg stepped forward. 'No tricks, Crowley. You tried to take my soul and failed. That is on you. Our deal still stands.' She glanced around the pub. 'Unless you want to show the world how you honour your contracts.'

Crowley's face twisted in rage, his form flickering in the firelight. 'This isn't over,' he spat, his voice a low, dangerous growl. 'I'll have what's owed to me, one way or another. I'll find you wherever you run to. No realm is beyond me.'

Crowley turned before Kitty or Peg could react, disappearing into the shadows. The *Necronomicon* remained on the table, untouched, its dark cover glinting in the flickering light.

Kitty turned to Peg, who was now panting, the light around her fading. 'Are you okay?'

Peg nodded, though her expression seemed strained. 'I'm fine. But we need to leave.'

Kitty grabbed the *Necronomicon*. Together, they

hurried out, the heavy oak door creaking shut behind them. The frozen night air hit them like a wave as they stepped outside, the fog swirling around them. She glanced back at the tavern, half expecting Crowley to storm after them, but the streets remained quiet. The oppressive feeling of the Serpent's Coil lifted, replaced by London's familiar aromas and sounds.

'Peg...' Kitty began, her voice soft. 'What was that in there? What happened?'

Peg exhaled, her breath visible in the cold air. 'My Light was promised to another long ago, someone far more powerful than any human, mage or otherwise.'

Kitty nodded, though her mind still swirled with questions. There would be time to understand it all later. Right now, they had what they came for.

'Let's go,' Kitty said, pulling her shawl tighter around her shoulders. 'We need to get back to the pyramid.'

Kitty and Peg moved through the fog-laden streets of London, the *Necronomicon* clutched in Kitty's hands. Taking a deep breath, she opened the book and recited the words Dr Dee had told them, the ancient language flowing from her lips like a song. The air around them crackled with energy, the ground trembling as the spell took hold.

A swirling vortex of light and shadow formed before them. Kitty's heart raced as the portal opened, the way back to their world shimmering just beyond the veil.

'Ready?' Kitty asked, her voice shaking.

Peg nodded, her eyes locked on the portal. 'Let's go.'

Shit! Lulu whispered.

Chapter 17

The Staff of Souls

Nothing happened.

Panic gripped Gemma. 'Are you thinking of the island, of the pyramid?'

'Yes,' Barbara answered.

'Yes,' Delf echoed.

Still nothing happened.

They continued for two minutes before Gemma let go and screamed.

'Why isn't it working?'

Barbara placed her hand on Gemma's shoulder. 'Maybe our task isn't completed yet.'

'Yes,' Delf added. 'The old man said the staff would take us back when we'd completed our task. There must be something else we need to do.'

'Shit!' Gemma said. 'So what now?'

'We get off this mountain,' Barbara replied.

The cold bite of the air faded as they descended, each step taking them farther from the sacred altar and the eerie presence of the creatures. The ancient staff, the weapon that could tip the balance in their war against The Soulless, was slung over Barbara's shoulder, its power still humming in a low, steady pulse.

As they pressed onward, the terrain changed. What had been a snow-capped, jagged landscape gave way to rocky paths and patches of dense, dark forest. Mist clung to the ground like a living thing, swirling around their ankles and making each step dangerous and uncertain. Every sound seemed amplified—the crunch of gravel, the distant calls of birds, the sighing wind through the branches. The tension in the air was thick, an unspoken understanding that danger still lurked, waiting just out of sight.

'We should find shelter,' Delf said, his voice gruff as he studied the dense forest ahead. His keen eyes flicked between the trees, always searching, always calculating.

'We need food and water,' Gemma added. 'A night out in the open like this is asking for trouble.'

Barbara nodded, her gaze drifting to the sky, now streaked with the deep hues of twilight. The sinking sun cast long shadows over the forest, turning the once beautiful landscape into a labyrinth of darkness and uncertainty. As they descended into the misty wilderness, the dense canopy above seemed to swallow the last of the daylight, leaving them in an oppressive, dim gloom.

The staff at Barbara's back felt heavy, not just in weight but in purpose. The sense of being hunted had never left her since their encounter with the creatures. It lingered in every breath and step, a constant reminder that they were unsafe. The beasts had been driven away for now, but they would return. Next time, they would be stronger.

Delf led the way, his footsteps almost silent despite the uneven terrain. Gemma followed, scanning the underbrush, alert for movement, her thoughts never far from Ella and Andrew.

It wasn't long before they found a small, natural cave tucked into the side of a rocky outcrop. The opening was narrow, just wide enough for one person to slip through at a time, but it opened up into a larger chamber that was dry and, more importantly, out of sight from the main path.

'This will do for the night,' Delf said, crouching near the entrance. 'We'll rest here, but we must keep watch.'

Barbara slid the staff from her shoulder and set it against the wall, the faint hum of its power still pulsing through the air. She could feel it, almost like it had a heartbeat, a living thing waiting to be used.

'What do we have to do before we can leave?' Gemma asked, sitting near the small fire Delf had created using a green spark from his fingers. The warmth was a welcome comfort, but it did little to chase away the chill that had settled in her bones.

'I don't know,' Barbara replied.

Gemma looked at her. 'Ella believes in you, Barbara, and so do we. You'll get us back to the island.'

'Your kind words warm my heart,' Barbara said. 'I'm not sure if I deserve them.'

Delf waved his hand at the flames, and they increased. 'You listened to our stories the other night. – why don't you tell us yours? It might help us settle in this strange place.'

Barbara nodded. 'I am a Valkyrie, born from the realms of myth and legend, destined to serve Odin and collect the souls of the bravest warriors to bring them to Valhalla. For centuries, I stood alongside my sisters, guardians of the fallen, guiding them to their eternal battle and feast, preparing them for Ragnarok. My wings, vast and shimmering with ethereal light, once soared over battlefields stained with blood and courage. I have seen countless lives end and countless heroes rise. But I have left all that behind—for a purpose far greater than I had ever known.

'In the beginning, I was like all my sisters, born from the essence of battle and the divine will of Odin. I revelled in the glory of combat, the clang of swords, the cries of warriors meeting their fate. Valhalla was my home, my eternal duty. Every day in Asgard felt like a dream, and the mead halls roared with the songs of warriors every night. We Valkyries took pride in our duty, but something was always missing for me. Unlike my sisters, who found purpose solely in their eternal task, I wondered what existed beyond the cycle of life and death.

'I remember watching the battles of mortals, not just with a sense of duty, but with curiosity. The lives they led before death intrigued me—their struggles, their love, their hatred, and their sense of purpose outside war. I started asking questions, something my sisters never did. I would speak to the souls we brought to Valhalla, asking about their lives before the battle that claimed them. Slowly, I realised there was more to existence than preparing for the world's end.

'I didn't know it then, but that curiosity, that need to know more, was the first step toward leaving Valhalla. That's when Ella summoned me to help her against the Institute—an organisation that sought control over realms and beings far beyond their understanding. They captured Elementals, beings from different dimensions, bending them to their will. I had heard of these beings before, creatures of light, fire, air, and shadow that stumbled into the mortal world through forgotten portals. I had never considered them much until I realised the Institute's reach wasn't limited to Earth. They were digging into realms they didn't belong in, including those connected to Valhalla.

'At first, it was just a curiosity. But as I listened more, I heard of the devastation they wrought, imprisoning creatures that should never have been caged, draining their essence for their own dark purposes. I felt a rage I had not known in centuries. This was more than just mortal ambition. It was blasphemy.

'Ella's struggle became clear to me. She wasn't just fighting to protect her world. She was battling to preserve all realms, to stop the Institute from upsetting the balance of life and death, time and space. I had a choice. I could continue my duties in Valhalla, ensuring the warriors were prepared for Ragnarok. Or I could take a stand in a fight that transcended the battle between gods and giants.

'I chose the latter.'

Gemma touched the Valkyrie's arm. 'Ella told me how you helped her. We will always be grateful to you for that.'

Barbara nodded. 'It is an honour and privilege to serve your daughter, Gemma Finn.'

'But,' Delf said. 'Didn't you change your name when you left Valhalla to go to Earth?'

'Yes,' Barbara answered. 'I wanted a new name for a new life in a new world. I was Sigrun no more.'

As the emerald fire crackled in the cave, exhaustion overwhelmed them. Delf, ever vigilant, took the first watch while Gemma and Barbara settled into an uneasy sleep. The forest outside was still, but every rustle of leaves and snap of a twig created unease.

They rose before dawn, with the dim light of pre-morning casting everything in a grey haze.

Gemma's mouth was dry, and her guts grumbled. But

she ignored them, focusing on something else. 'We should try with the staff again.'

Barbara agreed. They gripped the staff together, thinking of the island and the pyramids. Gemma pictured being with her daughter and husband. Barbara imagined seeing Gisela again. Delf thought of his friend Agrius.

They never moved.

Gemma let go and sighed. 'Let's keep moving.'

They set out, driven by a shared urgency. The further they travelled from the mountain, the more the landscape transformed. The dense forest gave way to rolling hills dotted with strange, towering stones, some carved with the intricate designs of ancient cultures. They entered another sacred area, but this one felt wrong, a sense of something primaeval and malevolent watching them.

Delf paused, his brow furrowing as he studied the stones. 'These aren't just markers. They're warnings.'

Barbara noticed the oppressive energy that pressed down on them as they walked. The staff at her back grew warmer, as if sensing the danger nearby. She exchanged a look with Gemma, who nodded, her hand resting on the dagger Seraphina had given her.

'I don't like this,' she said. 'Something's not right.'

They continued, cautious, as they wound their way through the stone pillars. The mist had thickened again, swirling around them in dense clouds, making it hard to see more than a few feet ahead. It was eerily quiet - a silence that made the hairs on the back of Barbara's neck stand on end.

Then, without warning, Delf stopped dead in his tracks, his body rigid. 'Do you hear that?'

Barbara strained to listen. At first, she heard nothing but

the muffled sound of their breathing. Then she caught it—a low, guttural growl echoing through the mist.

Something moved nearby.

'Get ready,' Delf hissed, drawing his blade.

They formed a tight circle, backs to each other, scanning the haze for any sign of movement. The growling grew louder, closer, and Barbara's grip tightened on the staff. The mist thickened, swirling faster, and shadows flickered just beyond the edge of their vision.

Then, from the haze, they came.

Creatures, tall and skeletal, their skin stretched tight over bony frames, eyes glowing with evil light. These were different from the other monsters—more feral, more savage. Their long limbs ended in sharp claws, and their mouths filled with rows of jagged teeth.

Barbara's muscles tensed as a beast lunged at them, moving with terrifying speed. Delf was the first to react, his blade slicing through the air to meet the creature's attack. The two clashed with a bone-rattling force, Delf's strength holding the creature at bay.

Gemma wasn't far behind, her blade flashing at the creatures. But there were too many of them, and they were coming from all sides. Barbara raised the staff, its power surging through her. The puma's head at the top glowed, and with a flick of her wrist, a bolt of energy shot out, striking a creature in the chest. It let out a deafening screech as it disintegrated into ash, but for every one that fell, two more took its place.

'We can't hold them off forever!' Gemma shouted, her voice strained with effort as she fought off another attacker.

Barbara felt the staff's power, but it was draining her with each use. They needed a way out and fast.

'Run!' Delf barked, slashing through a creature. 'Get to the stones!'

Barbara turned and sprinted toward the nearest pillar, the others following behind. The things gave chase, their guttural growls growing louder as they closed in on them.

The moment they reached the stones, something strange happened. The creatures stopped, their glowing eyes flickering with confusion. They paced at the edge of the stone circle, snarling and snapping, but they didn't cross the boundary.

'What's happening?' Gemma panted, her chest heaving as she stared at the beasts beyond the stones.

Barbara glanced around. 'The stones. They're a barrier.'

Delf wiped the sweat from his brow, his eyes narrowing. 'A barrier or a trap?'

They didn't have time to figure it out. The monsters grew more agitated, pacing the perimeter of the stone circle, testing the boundary. They wouldn't stay back forever.

Barbara studied their surroundings. The carvings on the stones were like the ones they'd seen before—symbols of the old gods, protective runes meant to ward off evil. But there was something more, something she hadn't noticed before.

'There's a pattern,' she said, nearing a stone. 'Look at the way these symbols are aligned. It's a path.'

Delf and Gemma exchanged a glance before stepping closer to examine the markings. Sure enough, the stones marked a distinct path, a series of symbols that led deeper into the mist.

'It's guiding us,' Barbara declared, her voice filled with wonder and apprehension. 'This isn't just a barrier. It's a path to something.'

Gemma looked sceptical. 'Or it's leading us into a trap.'

'Do we have a choice?' Delf asked. 'Either we take the path or stay here and wait for those things to break through.'

Barbara nodded. 'We follow it.'

With no other option, they set off, the mist swirling around them, the creatures still pacing at the edges of the stone circle. The staff pulsed with energy in Barbara's hand, guiding her forward. Every step was heavy, each symbol they passed humming with ancient power.

They walked for what felt like hours, the haze becoming thicker, the world growing more surreal with each passing moment. The path twisted and turned, leading them deeper into the unknown until they emerged into a wide clearing, seeing a massive stone structure, its walls covered in intricate carvings. The surrounding air buzzed with power, and at its centre was a doorway—dark and foreboding.

'This is it,' Barbara whispered. 'The next step.'

Gemma's hand tightened on her blade. 'Whatever's in there, it won't be friendly.'

Delf nodded. 'Then we face it together.'

They stepped through the doorway.

Chapter 18

Invasion

Veronica Venus had her best sleep in an age. She woke only once, glancing at Catherine's peaceful face as she slumbered beside her. In the night's stillness, she hoped her daughter was coming to terms with the time missed during her coma, though she knew it would be a long, delicate process. Catherine had lost years while the world around her had continued without her. It was a burden Veronica wished she could take from her.

Veronica slipped out of the tent, the breeze brushing against her skin. The island was quiet, save for the occasional whisper of wind through the trees. She moved towards the makeshift toilet Seraphina had constructed. Seraphina had been using most of her magic to keep the island hidden from the human world, especially from the ever-looming threat of the Institute, but she'd also built the facilities they needed with it.

As Veronica sat, the cold biting at her legs, her mind drifted to the others. Ella and the rest of the group had left earlier to explore the pyramid. They hadn't expected them back until morning, but Veronica couldn't shake the feeling that something was stirring, something dangerous. She tried to keep her thoughts calm, but with each passing day, it became harder to ignore the looming question: what would happen when they departed from the island? Where could she and Catherine go to escape the Institute?

As she finished and exited the small enclosure, she noticed the centaur standing nearby, staring into the sky with an expression that mirrored her unease.

'Can't you sleep, Agrius?' she asked, her voice soft but tinged with curiosity.

Agrius turned to her, his equine body shifting in the moonlight. 'The forest is magnificent,' he replied, deep and contemplative. 'It reminds me of Folio and my adventures with the other Centaurs and Heracles.'

Veronica smiled despite the weight in her chest. 'Even after everything I've seen, it's still hard to believe that the myths and legends we grew up with are real.'

Agrius regarded her with thoughtful eyes. 'These are things you learned while working for the Institute?'

She nodded. 'Mainly, yes.'

He stepped closer, his hooves crunching on the leaves. 'Seraphina told me much about them, and none of it was good.'

'No,' Veronica admitted, her face hardening. 'It wasn't.'

'And this is why you are no longer with them?'

Veronica's gaze flicked towards the tent where Catherine still slept. 'Thankfully, I came to my senses.'

'Ella Finn changed your mind?' Agrius asked, his tone less a question and more an acknowledgement.

Veronica nodded. 'She had a big hand in that. She's remarkable.'

Agrius raised his head, eyes drawn to the stars that peeked through the canopy. 'She is a star who fell into this world to help humans and Elementals. She can change things for the good of all.'

'You believe that?' Veronica asked, intrigued by his faith.

'Don't you?' Agrius asked.

She stared at the night sky, seeing a shimmer—Seraphina's magical barrier, which hummed, providing a subtle, almost comforting buzz in the background.

'Something needs to change,' Veronica replied. 'Otherwise, the Institute and similar organisations will start a war over acquiring and exploiting Elementals.'

'Ella told me some Elementals can repair the damage to the planet caused by humans. Is that true?'

Veronica shrugged. 'I don't know, but the Light inside Elementals can cure human illness.'

'We are on the cusp of something great or terrible,' Agrius said.

She agreed. 'I wonder if whatever is inside that pyramid will play a part in that.'

Agrius nodded, and they stood for a minute. Veronica was about to return to the tent when a strange noise distracted her. A distant whirring—like the beating of mechanical wings—grew louder by the second.

'Do you hear that?' Agrius asked, his body tense as his sharp eyes scanned the sky.

Veronica's stomach sank as the realisation hit her. 'Seraphina's barrier... it's down.'

Agrius's head tilted. 'The humans are here.'

Veronica gasped. 'It's the Institute!' she shouted, rushing to the tent. 'Get up, Cat!'

Catherine remained still, her serene face a painful reminder of the years lost to the coma.

Veronica grabbed her arms and shook her. 'Catherine!'

Her daughter's eyes snapped open wide and filled with confusion. 'What? What is it?'

'We have to go,' Veronica said, her voice steady despite the growing dread. The helicopters were closer now, the sound of their blades slicing through the air like approaching death. 'The Institute is here.'

Catherine scrambled to her feet, disoriented but following her mother's urgency.

'They'll be here soon,' Agrius said.

Veronica peered into the trees, her eyes searching for movement, but the forest remained still, a peaceful sea of green. 'Where's Gisela?'

'I haven't seen the dragon for hours,' Agrius replied, his brow furrowing in concern.

Catherine's voice wavered. 'What do we do?'

Agrius extended his hand. 'Come, I will hide you in the forest.'

Veronica's instincts kicked in, her mind calculating their best chance of survival. 'Take us to the pyramid.'

Agrius nodded, his muscles tensing as he prepared to race through the trees. 'Hold on.'

Veronica and Catherine climbed onto his back, their grip firm as Agrius surged into the forest, his powerful strides making the ground disappear beneath them. The wind whipped through Veronica's hair as the darkness closed around them, thick with the scent of moss and earth. Her heart pounded, not just from the speed, but from the fear gnawing at her mind—would they make it in time?

The helicopters grew louder, their searchlights piercing through the canopy in streaks of white. The air thrummed with the sound of rotors and engines, mechanical and alien, in the untouched wilderness. Agrius ducked and weaved through the dense trees with a grace that belied his massive size. Veronica felt Catherine's trembling arms around her waist, and she squeezed her daughter's hand, trying to offer reassurance despite her growing dread.

'They're getting closer!' Catherine cried, her voice cracking over the roar of the helicopters.

She glanced over her shoulder. The beams of light were sweeping through the forest, catching flashes of movement. Any moment now, they would be spotted.

A sudden crash echoed through the trees, and Veronica struggled to breathe. The ground shook beneath Agrius's hooves as something enormous barrelled behind them.

'What is that?' Veronica shouted, her eyes wide as she tried to make sense of the noise.

Before Agrius could answer, a massive shape burst through the underbrush—a towering mechanical monstrosity, its metal limbs gleaming in the helicopter lights. The Institute had sent soldiers and machines—hunters designed to track and capture. Its red eyes locked onto them, letting out a metallic roar.

'Hold tight!' Agrius yelled, his pace quickening as he dodged through the trees.

Veronica's breath came in sharp gasps as they raced through the forest. The machine crashed after them, smashing through trees and brush with relentless force. The scent of burning metal filled the air as its joints sparked with each movement, a smell that mixed with the earthy tang of nature.

'We won't outrun that thing!' Catherine cried, panic creeping into her voice.

Veronica glanced back at the pursuing machine, its steel

claws tearing into the ground with each step. She grasped for a solution, anything that could slow it down.

But there was nothing.

Agrius strained his muscles as he pushed harder, navigating the dense foliage with incredible speed. But the machine wasn't slowing down. It was closing the gap, its mechanical limbs tearing through the forest.

Then, a low growl rumbled from the shadows, and out of nowhere, Gisela appeared, her scales glinting in the light. With a frightening roar, she launched herself at the invader, her powerful jaws clamping down on its metal frame. They tumbled through the trees, Elemental flesh and human-machine screaming in the night.

Agrius didn't hesitate. He galloped away. Veronica gripped onto him and looked back, watching the dragon and the machine locked in a deadly battle, sparks soaring as Gisela's fiery breath scorched the machine's metal skin.

Her heart went out to the dragon, wondering if they should stop to help the Elemental.

Then something smashed into them, and they went flying.

Agrius hit a tree as Veronica and Catherine let go, falling in opposite directions. Veronica's training kicked in, jumping up to aid her daughter, stopping when she saw the armed Institute soldiers heading for them.

Veronica's pulse quickened as she scrambled to her feet, eyes darting between Catherine and the approaching invaders. The sound of their boots filled her with a sickening dread. She grabbed Catherine's arm and tugged her towards the cover of a tree.

'Catherine, run!' Veronica shouted, her voice cutting through the chaos. Her daughter, though dazed and dizzy, reacted quickly. With a glance at her mother, she bolted toward the dense shadows of the trees.

Veronica turned back to face the soldiers. She had no weapons, no magic to protect her—only the hard-earned skills and instincts she'd developed during her time at the Institute. The attackers advanced, their tactical lights slicing through the dark. She knew their tactics. They'd fan out, surround her, and take her down. They wouldn't kill her unless they had to, but she wasn't planning to give them the chance to capture her alive.

'Stay down, monster!' one of the soldiers barked at Agrius, who rose to his feet, still recovering from the fall.

Veronica glanced at Agrius. He was strong but injured. He wouldn't be able to fight them all. She needed to buy them time.

'Agrius, get to the pyramid,' she hissed. 'Take Catherine. I'll hold them off.'

He hesitated, his large frame tense with indecision. 'Veronica, I...'

'Go!' she ordered, her voice firm.

With a nod, he turned and knelt for Catherine, who ran to him from her hiding place in the trees. With her, he galloped towards the pyramid, weaving through the trees with Catherine clinging to his back. Veronica's ribs ached as she watched them disappear into the trees, but she knew she had to stay focused.

The soldiers advanced closer. Veronica heard the faint clicks of their gear, the low murmur of orders being exchanged. She crouched behind a tree, her breath steady, her mind racing for a plan. They were coming for her, and she had to think fast.

The forest was dark and dense—her best advantage. Years of fieldwork had taught her how to move silently and use the environment to her favour. She'd have to stay one step ahead of them. Footsteps crunched nearby. She held her breath, waiting for the soldier to get closer. When the moment was right, she darted from behind the tree, snatched a thick branch from the ground, and swung it hard at the back of his head. He collapsed with a grunt, his helmet offering only partial protection from the blow.

Veronica grabbed his rifle and searched him for anything useful. A small combat knife and a radio. She yanked the blade from its sheath, clipped it to her belt, and switched off the radio—no point in letting them track her movements that way.

She darted back into the shadows, weaving between trees and using the terrain to her advantage. The soldiers would spread out, combing the area, but they were trained to stick to patterns and follow orders. She could disrupt that.

A faint noise—a twig snapping—made her freeze. Another soldier was close. Too close. She pressed her back against a large tree, barely breathing, listening to the invader approaching.

As soon as he passed her, she moved. Swift and silent, she came up behind him, wrapped an arm around his throat, and dragged him into the underbrush. He struggled, but she tightened her grip, choking off his air until he went limp.

Veronica let him go, grabbing the radio from his vest and tossing it deep into the woods. They'd find it eventually, but it would confuse them for a few precious minutes.

The helicopters circled above, their searchlights sweeping everywhere. Veronica's mind buzzed with decisions. They were closing in, and she had little time.

She darted through the forest, searching for the pyramid. The looming stone structure rose above the treetops, a dark silhouette against the sky. She knew Catherine and Agrius would head there; that was where she needed to be.

Then, a low rumble shook the ground beneath her. Veronica stumbled, her hand shooting out to brace herself against a tree. The sound grew louder, and she saw something massive moving toward her through the foliage.

A mechanical beast—a hunter drone—was crashing through the forest, its metal limbs gleaming in the helicopter lights. It was a terrifying creation, built for one purpose: to track and capture. Its red eyes scanned the trees, locking onto her position.

Her stomach dropped. There was no way she could outrun it, not in a straight line. But maybe she could outsmart it.

She sprinted toward the nearest ridge, her legs burning with the effort. The drone followed, crashing through the trees behind her with relentless speed. Veronica's breath came in sharp gasps as she dodged through the underbrush, hoping to throw it off her trail.

She reached the ridge, a steep drop-off that led down into a rocky ravine. She jumped over the edge without hesitation, grabbing a thick vine to slow her descent. The drone, too heavy and too large to stop in time, barrelled past her and plunged over the ridge, smashing into the rocks below.

Veronica hung there for a moment, her chest heaving, listening to the drone's dying whirrs as it struggled to move. Its red eyes flickered once, then went dark.

She pulled herself up to solid ground, her arms trembling. But there was no time to rest. She needed to reach the others.

As she neared the structure, she heard gunfire. Her heart raced as she ran to the base of the pyramid, where

Agrius and Catherine were pinned behind a pile of rubble. The soldiers had reached them, and bullets ricocheted off the stone around them.

Veronica dropped to her stomach and crawled through the brush, moving toward the attackers. Three advanced, their weapons trained on Agrius and Catherine's position. Veronica steadied herself, her muscles tensing as she prepared to act. In one fluid motion, she lunged forward, knife in hand. She took down the nearest soldier, his body crumpling before the others even realised what had happened.

The remaining two soldiers whirled around, their weapons raised, but Veronica was already moving. She smashed the rifle from one and tackled him to the ground, delivering a quick blow to his temple that knocked him unconscious. The last soldier hesitated, his gun wavering as he glanced between Veronica and the fallen men. In that split second, Agrius charged forward, knocking the soldier off his feet with a powerful kick from his hooves.

Silence fell over the forest, broken only by the distant hum of helicopters.

Veronica stood, wiping the sweat from her brow. She looked at Agrius and Catherine, relief flooding her chest.

'We need to move,' Veronica said. 'More will be coming.'

Agrius nodded, helping Catherine to her feet. She appeared shaken but unhurt. Veronica took her daughter's hand, squeezing it. Together, they marched up the pyramid's steps, scanning the sky for any sign of more soldiers. But for now, they had a moment of respite.

As they reached the top, Veronica caught her breath. The helicopters were still circling but kept their distance, likely waiting for reinforcements.

'We'll find Ella and the others and figure out what's inside this pyramid,' Veronica said, quiet but resolute. 'And we'll use it to stop them. This isn't over.'

Catherine looked at her mother, her face filled with fear and determination. 'What if we can't?'

Veronica met her gaze, her jaw set. 'We will.'

Chapter 19

The Return

Ella thought she was falling into the sun, dazzled by light and heat. Everything shimmered around her, her skin tingling and her ears howling with thunder.

Then she hit the ground and twisted onto her shoulder. A throbbing pain shot through her arms and sides as her breathing pounded her lungs. The Book of All Life was in one hand, the Eye of the Forgotten in the other. A twisting illumination dissipated, and she realised where she was: inside the pyramid.

But where was her father?

She put the Book of All Life and the Eye of the Forgotten in her bag on her back and got up. 'Dad!' she shouted.

'Over here, Ella,' he replied.

He stepped out of the shadows, hanging onto Lyssa.

'The transportation has weakened him,' she said.

She ran to her father, removing the backpack and helping him to sit. 'Are you okay?'

He smiled at her. 'I'll be fine.'

'Ella!' someone yelled.

She turned to see her mother rushing towards her, followed by Barbara and Delf.

'What happened?' Gemma asked.

Andrew hugged his wife. 'We went to ancient Stonehenge and then to the Realm of The Soulless.' He nodded at Ella's bag. 'We brought a present.'

Barbara narrowed her eyes. 'Who is the girl?'

'That's Lyssa,' Ella replied. 'She helped us get back here. What happened to you?'

'The stone you touched transported us to Giza in Egypt,' Gemma answered.

Ella sighed. 'I'm sorry.'

'Don't be, child,' Barbara said. 'We also returned with a gift.' She lifted her arm. 'This is the Staff of Souls. It can kill The Soulless.'

Ella's heart settled, not punching against her chest anymore. Then she saw a light coming towards them. 'What's that?'

Everyone turned, readying for a fight.

'Hello, friends,' Seraphina said. The glow emanated from an orb in her hand. Callisto strode by her side. She looked at Ella. 'Best not to touch that rune stone again.'

Ella grinned. 'Where did it send you, and what are you holding?'

'We travelled to the realm between life and death,' Callisto answered.

Ella gasped while her parents gripped each other's hands.

'We encountered the Warden of Souls, and this is his heart,' Seraphina added.

Barbara moved towards the shimmering orb. 'We know of the Warden of Souls in Valhalla, a creature of unimaginable power who controls life and death.' She held out the Staff of Souls. 'It is rumoured that the Warden once owned this staff.' She turned to Ella. 'What did you bring back with you?'

Ella removed the dark, glassy sphere from her bag. 'This is the Eye of the Forgotten. With it, you can see into the hearts of any living creatures, to strip away their souls, leaving only emptiness behind.'

'All three items are linked to souls and the defeat of The Soulless,' Lyssa said.

Seraphina studied the girl's face. 'Where are you from?'

Ella explained how they met. 'We wouldn't have got back without her.'

'How do you know so much about these objects and The Soulless?' Seraphina asked.

The girl's eyes sparkled. 'I was a prisoner of The Soulless. I led Ella and her father to the Eye of the Forgotten.'

'Why?' Seraphina questioned.

'Why?' Lyssa replied. 'To escape that place.' She pointed at the artefacts. 'You need all three of those to defeat The Soulless.'

'Excellent,' Callisto said.

Seraphina glanced between the orb she held and the other relics. 'How will they defeat The Soulless?'

Lyssa narrowed her eyes. 'The Staff of Souls contains the energy to hurt The Soulless. The Eye of the Forgotten allows the user to identify any Soulless hiding inside a human form. You use the heart from the Warden of Souls to bind The Soulless. But they are not enough.'

'Why?' Ella asked.

Lyssa answered. 'Because you need one last object to kill The Soulless.'

'Is this it?' a voice said behind them.

The group turned to see Kitty and Peg approaching, with Kitty holding a small book.

'Is that what I think it is?' Barbara asked.

Kitty grinned. 'Well, if you're thinking about the Book of the Dead, then yes.'

Seraphina nearly dropped the orb. 'The *Necronomicon?*'

Peg nodded. 'We stole it from a mage in Victorian London.'

Barbara moved forward. 'It's no coincidence that the rune sent us to where these objects resided. It knew what we needed to defeat The Soulless.'

Ella gazed at the stone she'd touched, peering at the moving symbols. 'It?'

'Yes,' Lyssa said. 'The Idol of The Soulless is a living thing.'

'Why would *it* send us for these items?' Gemma asked.

'Because,' Lyssa added. 'It is a prisoner like me. If you defeat The Soulless, you will free the soul trapped inside the Idol.'

Ella felt the pull of the Idol, a whispering voice calling to her. 'Whose soul is it?'

Lyssa shrugged. 'I don't know.'

'What do we do now?' Peg asked.

They stood in silence. Then the walls trembled, and dust fell from the ceiling.

'That's an explosion,' Andrew Finn said.

Everybody froze, hearing the sounds of hooves approaching. Agrius rode into the chamber with Veronica and Catherine Venus on his back.

'The island is under attack,' Veronica announced.

'By who?' Gemma said.

'The Institute,' Ella answered.

Veronica nodded. 'We only escaped by the skin of our teeth.'

There were more noises outside, and the pyramid trembled again.

Seraphina shook her head. 'The mystical barrier I placed over the island must have collapsed when I was away.'

The group stood silently, the air tense and heavy with anticipation as the pyramid trembled from the explosions. Dust rained down, coating their clothes as distant gunfire echoed through the walls. Ella felt the energy beneath her feet. Her thoughts raced as she processed everything. The artefacts they'd gathered were powerful, but now it was clear their fight wasn't just against The Soulless but also the Institute.

Barbara's gaze swept the room. 'The Institute is relentless. They won't stop until they have all of us.'

Veronica looked up, still helping Catherine from Agrius' back. 'We barely escaped. They came prepared. Heavy artillery, elite soldiers. They're tearing through the island.'

Ella swallowed, her fingers brushing against the bag that held the Eye of the Forgotten and the Book of All Life. She couldn't let them fall into the Institute's hands. Not after all they'd gone through.

'They've come for Ella,' Gemma said

Veronica's eyes hardened. 'They've searched for this island for years. It's a goldmine of knowledge, relics, power —everything the Institute covets. But now, with what we've uncovered, they'll stop at nothing to take it all.'

'They don't know about The Soulless,' Ella added. 'Their goals aren't about them. They see us as rogue elements, threats to their authority.'

'So we're dealing with two enemies,' Peg said, glancing around. 'The Institute, and The Soulless. Fantastic.'

Ella glanced at her mother and father. They'd faced the Institute before, but not like this. This time, they were pinned inside a pyramid with an army bearing down on them and an ancient evil lurking in the shadows.

'What do we do?' Ella asked, her voice quieter than she intended.

Barbara's face hardened. 'We don't let the Institute win. We've come too far for that.'

Seraphina stood straighter, the orb containing the Warden of Souls' heart still glowing in her hand. 'We need to keep them from advancing further. The relics we gathered are too dangerous in their hands.'

'I can sense their forces closing in,' Callisto said. 'They'll break through soon.'

Ella glanced at her friends and her family. They'd fought hard and uncovered many secrets, but now the looming threat felt overwhelming. How could they fight against such a relentless enemy?

Barbara interrupted her thoughts. 'We split up. Some of us hold them off, keep them distracted. The rest will ensure the relics stay out of their hands.'

'I agree,' Delf said, stepping forward. 'And we need to make sure they never get to Ella.'

Veronica nodded at Catherine. 'Agrius, take Cat to safety. You'll do more good protecting her.'

He agreed. 'I'll escort her to the far side of the pyramid. We'll find shelter.'

Peg and Delf moved near the entrance. 'We'll hold them off as long as possible,' Delf declared. 'They won't seize this place without a fight.'

Veronica turned to Ella, concern etched into her face.

'You and your parents need to keep those artefacts safe. If the Institute gets their hands on them…'

'We won't let that happen,' Andrew Finn said.

Barbara kept the Staff of Souls as Ella placed the other objects into her bag with the Book of All Life. It wasn't as heavy as she expected as she hung it on her shoulder, but there was a different weight over her now, the ancient relics humming with power. She met her father's gaze and nodded.

Another explosion shook the ground, closer this time, and Ella knew they were running out of time.

Barbara motioned for Ella, Lyssa, Gemma, and Andrew to follow her. 'We'll head deeper into the pyramid and find somewhere secure to hide the relics. The rest of you—keep them occupied.'

The group moved swiftly. Delf, Kitty, and Veronica headed toward the entrance to prepare for the onslaught of soldiers. Agrius, with Catherine and Peg, disappeared down one of the side tunnels. Seraphina and Callisto split off in the opposite direction, searching for the best place to make their stand.

Ella followed behind Barbara, Lyssa, and her parents as they moved deeper into the pyramid's labyrinthine corridors. The walls closed in on them as the sounds of explosions outside intensified. The Institute was coming and fast.

They reached a large chamber filled with carvings and ancient statues, the air thick with the scent of dust and stone. Barbara stopped, scanning the room.

'We can't linger here long,' Andrew said, his voice tense. 'They'll find us, eventually.'

'We won't stay,' Barbara replied. 'We're just hiding the relics. We'll fight them on our terms, not theirs.'

Ella hesitated. 'And The Soulless? What if they appear?'

'We'll deal with them if they do,' Barbara replied. 'Right now, the Institute is the more immediate threat.'

They moved to one of the large statues, its hollow eyes staring down at them. Barbara pulled back a section of the stone base, revealing a small compartment beneath. 'Put your bag in there,' she instructed Ella.

Ella felt a strange reluctance to do it. She looked at Lyssa. 'Are we doing the right thing?'

The girl nodded. 'You can't let these humans get the only things capable of stopping The Soulless.'

Ella placed them inside the compartment, her hands shaking.

'Good,' Barbara said, closing the compartment. 'They won't find them here.'

The chamber fell silent, and for a moment, Ella heard the distant rumble of explosions and gunfire. Then, a new sound cut through the air—a steady, rhythmic beat of footsteps.

'They're coming,' Andrew announced.

Chapter 20

The Attack

The pyramid trembled as explosions reverberated across the island. Standing near the entrance, Delf tightened his grip on the warhammer his limited magic had created. The weapon hummed with a faint, almost imperceptible vibration, responding to his tension. Dust fell from the ceiling in tiny clouds, but he remained focused, eyes narrowed at the approaching Institute soldiers.

Behind him, Veronica and Kitty stood side by side, readying for the assault. They had no weapons, but Veronica's martial arts training would be her defence. Meanwhile, Kitty adjusted her gloves, the sharp claws hidden inside, ready to tear through armour if necessary.

Further inside the chamber, Agrius was pacing, his hooves clacking against the stone floor in agitation. Catherine Venus sat on his back, her eyes wide but determined. She glanced at Peg as the water sprite surveyed the chaos with a grim expression.

Seraphina and Callisto had moved to the chamber's far end, away from the entrance. Seraphina's hands glowed with a soft, golden light, and she was murmuring incantations under her breath, preparing for the inevitable confrontation. Callisto, her tall frame tense, was ready to die for her friends. The Institute would not imprison her again.

'More are coming,' Delf growled. His voice was deep, filled with ancient patience. He'd fought countless wars and seen more battles than any living creature could recount, yet today felt different. The stakes were higher than ever before. The Institute wasn't a typical enemy—they were calculating, methodical, and devoid of mercy. His scars from their experiments, both physical and emotional, would never leave him.

Kitty adjusted her stance. 'We should take the high ground. They'll be bottlenecked in the entrance, and we'll pick them off before they get too close.'

Veronica nodded in agreement, grabbing a handful of rocks from the dirt. 'Delf can hold the line. Agrius and I will flank from the sides.'

Delf released a deep grunt of approval. 'I'll smash anyone who gets through. No one's making it past us today.'

Veronica glanced at Kitty, her eyes softening for a moment. 'Stay close to Delf. You're quicker than any of us, but don't take unnecessary risks.'

Kitty flashed a toothy grin, her sharp teeth gleaming. 'No promises.'

Everybody regrouped in the main chamber, preparing for conflict. Delf remained near the entrance, a barrier against any soldiers that dared to approach. Kitty dashed to a shadowed corner, crouching low, her eyes glinting with anticipation. Veronica crawled onto a ledge, ready to hurl the stones at the intruders. Agrius trotted to the other side of the chamber, positioning himself for a pincer attack when the time was right.

An initial wave of Institute soldiers burst through the entrance with mechanical precision. They were well-armed, clad in black tactical gear, and moved in tight formation, their weapons raised. The pyramid's entrance had been breached, and now, the Institute was pouring in like a flood.

Veronica was the first to strike. A sharp stone hurled through the air, piercing the eye slit of the lead soldier's helmet. He dropped, his body crumpling as the others continued forward, undeterred. Before they could react, Kitty launched herself from the shadows, claws extended. She was on the nearest invader in a flash, tearing through his armour with a swift swipe. Her claws sank into his chest, and he collapsed with a gurgling cry. Another soldier turned, raising his weapon to fire, but Kitty ducked low, dodging the shots as she slashed at his legs, sending him crashing to the ground.

Agrius roared as he charged into the fray. His huge frame bulldozed into the remaining soldiers, his hooves stomping. Catherine clung to his back, her eyes wide as the Centaur trampled through the Institute forces. Agrius' powerful arms swung a massive stone, knocking invaders aside like rag dolls.

Peg summoned water from underground. It burst through the earth, swirling in the air before she sent it hurtling at the soldiers rushing towards them. The liquid hit them hard, forcing them back into their colleagues, tumbling like pins in a bowling alley.

But more followed behind them.

Veronica kept her vantage point, picking off invaders with her stones. Each throw was precise, aimed at weak points in their armour. The tide of soldiers was relentless, but her focus never wavered.

'Delf!' Agrius shouted as more soldiers poured in. 'Hold them off!'

Delf let out a guttural roar, swinging his warhammer with brutal efficiency. The first soldier that came too close was sent flying across the chamber, slamming into the wall with a sickening thud. Another lunged at Delf with a knife, but he blocked the attack and brought his hammer down, crushing the soldier's arm before finishing him with a single blow.

'More are coming!' Kitty yelled as she dodged a volley of gunfire. She leapt behind a pillar, just avoiding the spray of bullets.

Agrius snorted, his nostrils flaring as he kicked a soldier in the chest, sending him flying across the room. 'We need to thin their numbers!'

'I'm working on it,' Veronica said through gritted teeth, releasing another stone that found its mark in a soldier's throat.

Catherine climbed off Agrius and looked back toward Peg, her voice trembling. 'Peg, can you find more water?'

'I'll try,' Peg replied, but even though she focused her mind and body on searching the surrounding ground, no more water was underneath the pyramid.

Agrius stood in front of Peg and Catherine. 'No one's getting through.'

Seraphina and Callisto watched the battle unfold from a distance on the far side of the chamber. Seraphina's Light flickered with energy in her hands, but hiding the island had drained her. The soldiers were unyielding, but there was something more sinister at play, something she couldn't put her finger on.

'They're well-trained,' Callisto muttered.

Seraphina nodded, her brows furrowed in concentration. 'The Institute doesn't move without reason. They know what's at stake here.'

Callisto tilted her head, her sharp eyes scanning the enemy. 'They aren't just here for Ella, are they?'

Seraphina's expression darkened. 'They want control, to break us.'

Callisto surged forward, her claws flashing as she cut through the first line of invaders with surgical precision. Her movements were a deadly dance, each strike deliberate and calculated. Soldiers fell around her, unable to match her speed or skill.

Seraphina raised her hand, summoning a shield of light that blocked an incoming volley of gunfire. The bullets disintegrated as they hit the barrier, leaving the enemy stunned. Callisto took advantage of the distraction, slicing through the remaining soldiers. Her eyes gleamed with the thrill of the fight, but there was also a cold, unyielding determination behind her every movement.

Peg's face flickered with a strange light as she chanted an ancient spell. The words seemed to come alive in her mouth, each syllable carrying a weight far beyond anything she had ever spoken. The surrounding air hummed with power, the temperature in the room dropping as a cold wind swirled through the chamber.

Catherine shivered, hugging her cloak closer to her. 'What's she doing?'

Agrius glanced back at Peg, his eyes narrowing with concern. 'Something dangerous.'

Peg continued to chant, her voice rising in intensity. The ground trembled, and a dark, swirling mist formed around her. The soldiers approaching from the entrance hesitated, their steps faltering as the ominous energy grew.

'Whatever she's doing,' Kitty muttered, her claws dripping with blood, 'it's freaking them out.'

Delf grunted, his hammer crashing down on another soldier. 'Good.'

As Peg's chant reached its crescendo, the mist coalesced into a tangible form—an ancient, monstrous entity that towered over them. Its eyes glowed with an evil light, and its presence filled the room with an overwhelming sense of dread. The invaders, despite their training, froze in terror.

The creature let out a low, rumbling growl, its eyes locking onto the Institute forces. With a swipe of its massive arm, it sent a dozen soldiers hurtling across the chamber, their bodies crashing into the walls with bone-cracking force.

Catherine gasped, her hand flying to her mouth. 'What is that?'

'A water demon,' Agrius said, his eyes wide with awe and fear. 'Peg just summoned a demon.'

Peg whispered, trembling from the effort. She looked up at the creature, her eyes glazed with exhaustion. 'It will only last a few minutes, but it should be enough.'

The demon continued to wreak havoc on the Institute soldiers, tearing through their ranks. The tide of battle seemed to be in their favour.

Veronica leapt from her perch, landing next to Kitty. 'We need to regroup.'

Kitty wiped the blood from her claws. 'No kidding. They just keep coming. Was it like this when you worked for them?'

Veronica shook her head. 'Black has militarised them.'

'Black?' Kitty asked.

'Director Gideon Black,' Veronica replied. 'He's in charge of the Institute. Or he was when I left. Maybe the government replaced him with someone even more extreme.'

Delf let out a heavy sigh, his chest heaving with exertion. 'We've bought ourselves some time. But we can't hold them off forever.'

Agrius trotted over, his gaze fixed on Peg, now sitting on the ground, her head resting on her knees. Catherine knelt beside her with an arm around her waist.

'You did good, Peg,' Agrius said. 'But we need to move. The Institute won't stop until they get what they came for.'

Veronica looked at the far side of the chamber, where Seraphina and Callisto were finishing off the last of the soldiers. 'We must get to the lower levels. We might have a chance if we can hold them off long enough for Ella and the others to secure the relics and escape.'

'Is there another way out of the pyramid?' Kitty asked.

'I hope so,' Veronica answered.

Agrius nodded, his expression grim. 'Let's move.'

Before they could move, the ground rumbled again. Heavy footsteps echoed from the corridor leading to the pyramid's entrance.

'They're sending in reinforcements,' Callisto said.

Veronica's heart sank as she saw what was coming. More invaders—dozens of them—were marching towards the chamber, their weapons at the ready. But these weren't ordinary soldiers. They were larger, their armour thicker, and their faces obscured by metal masks that reflected no light. Behind them, a figure strode forward.

'I don't know whether to thank you or shoot you, Veronica,' Gideon Black said.

'You could just bugger off,' Veronica replied.

He didn't move. 'I could have lost my job because of you, Veronica.'

She grinned. 'Yet here you are.'

He returned her smile. 'Aren't you wondering how we knew you were here?'

She wanted to keep him talking, giving her time to think of a way out. 'Surprise me.'

Black shook his head, studying those in the chamber. 'It's a nice collection of freaks you have here, Veronica, but at least Catherine is well. But where are the Finns?'

Then it dawned on her. 'You put trackers on Ella's parents.'

'Not on them, Veronica – inside them.'

She sighed. 'You kept that quiet from me at the Institute.'

'With good reason,' he said. 'So I know they're here somewhere. Where's Ella and that magic book of hers?'

An explosion rattled the roof, sending debris tumbling down. Veronica thought she could use the distraction to get the others away until she remembered how efficient and ruthless the Institute was.

'What's happening outside?' she asked.

His expression darkened. 'One of the girl's monsters is proving harder to deal with than anticipated. It will just be a matter of time. Now tell me where Ella is, and I might let the rest of you live.'

Veronica didn't move. 'The Institute has had an upgrade since I left.'

'When you betrayed us,' he replied.

She dug her nails into her palms. 'You can't keep doing this, Gideon.'

'Doing what?'

'Capturing innocent creatures and experimenting on them. It's inhumane.'

A fire burned in his eyes. 'Innocent creatures? Inhumane?' He pointed at Catherine. 'Have you forgotten what these things did to your daughter?'

Seraphina stepped near Veronica, lowering her voice so the Director of the Institute couldn't hear her. 'We need rest to replenish our Light, but me, Peg and Delf have enough to fight a last stand.'

'No,' Veronica said. 'No more sacrifices.'

But what could they do against such overwhelming forces?

That thought burned inside her head when there was an explosion behind them.

Chapter 21

The Fight

Barbara's eyes hardened. 'We need to draw them away from here. They can't know what we've hidden.'

A surge of adrenaline rushed through Ella. 'What's the plan?'

Barbara glanced at her. 'We fight. We make them regret ever setting foot here.'

The footsteps grew louder and closer. Barbara lifted the Staff of Souls, its energy crackling. 'Stay close to us, Ella.'

The door to the chamber burst open, and a squad of Institute soldiers stormed in, their weapons raised. They froze for a split second upon seeing the group, but then moved into position, ready to strike. Barbara didn't hesitate. She thrust the Staff of Souls forward, sending a flash of energy toward the attackers. The lead man was thrown back, crashing into the wall with a sickening thud. The others opened fire, but Barbara deflected the bullets with the Staff, moving at an impossible speed.

Ella struggled to breathe as she watched the soldiers retreat.

'Stay low,' Barbara called, sending another wave of energy toward the enemy. 'We need to keep them off balance!'

Ella ducked behind a statue. Taking a deep breath, she removed a small blade from her belt. It wasn't much, but it was all she had. She peeked out, eyes locking on a soldier advancing on her father. Without thinking, she threw the knife. It hit the man's ungloved hand, causing him to drop his gun with a pained shout. Andrew seized the moment, grabbing the weapon and clubbing the soldier in the knee. He fell, and Andrew hit him again in the head.

Barbara moved with fluid precision, her staff crackling with energy as she sent waves of force that kept the bulk of the Institute soldiers at bay. Each strike was a calculated blow, knocking back invaders and creating bursts of light that disoriented their ranks. The air sizzled with power as she fought, holding the line with an unwavering focus.

But despite her efforts, a few of the soldiers slipped past her defence, their eyes locked onto the others in the chamber. They were well-trained, moving in formation as they closed in on Ella, Lyssa, Gemma, and Andrew.

'They're coming!' Ella shouted, backing up against a statue.

Andrew stepped in front of her. 'Stay behind me,' he said, his voice filled with protective authority. He blocked the first blow from a soldier's baton using the rifle with a swift parry, shoving the man away. But two more soldiers advanced, aiming their guns at them.

Gemma grabbed a rock from the ground, her breath in short gasps. She wasn't a fighter, but wouldn't stand by and do nothing. She hurled the stone at a soldier, hitting him in the face. He stumbled, giving Andrew the chance to kick him in the head.

'Ella, get back!' Gemma yelled, her eyes wide with fear as the remaining attacker aimed at her.

For a split second, time seemed to slow for Ella. She couldn't just watch as her family fought around her. She rushed forward, ignoring her mother's warning. She ducked low, avoiding a swipe from the nearest soldier, and punched into the back of his knee. He cried out in pain, dropping to the ground. Ella scrambled away as Lyssa moved in, her small frame belying her speed. Lyssa leapt at the fallen attacker. She kicked the weapon away and delivered a quick, precise blow to his throat, rendering him unconscious.

'Ella!' Lyssa called, her voice tight with adrenaline. 'Keep moving!'

Two more invaders broke through Barbara's defence, charging forward with batons raised. Andrew blocked one with the rifle, but the other lunged past him, swinging his weapon at Ella. She ducked, the baton missing her by inches.

Before she could react, he swung again, this time aiming for her legs. The impact caught her off guard, and she fell to the ground, pain shooting through her leg. She gasped, scrambling to get on her feet, but the soldier was on top of her, his club raised for another blow.

Just as it came down, Lyssa intercepted, tackling the man from the side and knocking him down. They struggled for control, but Lyssa moved like lightning, her hands a blur as she twisted the soldier's arm behind him and slammed his head into the ground. It was impressive, considering her slight frame.

Gemma, trembling but determined, grabbed a discarded gun and pointed it at the remaining invader. Her fingers shook. 'Stay back!' she shouted. The soldier hesitated, startled by the sudden display of resistance.

Andrew used the opening, smashing the rifle into the man's face. The soldier fell, clutching his head as Andrew towered over him. 'You should've stayed down,' Andrew muttered before knocking the man unconscious with the hilt of the weapon.

Gasping, Ella scrambled to her feet, wincing as her leg throbbed where the baton had struck. Her heart raced, but she was alive.

Barbara, her focus still on the attackers, glanced back for a brief second. 'Everyone all right?'

'We're okay!' Andrew shouted, scanning the room for more threats.

Ella nodded, her breath coming in ragged bursts. Her hands shook, energy coursing through her veins. She looked at Lyssa, who was on her feet, calm and composed despite the surrounding chaos.

'We're not out of this yet,' Lyssa said.

Gemma rushed over, pulling Ella into a quick embrace. 'Are you hurt?'

'I'm fine,' Ella assured her, though her leg still throbbed. She glanced at the doorway, where more soldiers could be heard approaching. 'But we have to move.'

Barbara's voice cut through the room. 'They're regrouping. We need to get out.'

Andrew nodded. 'We can't keep them off forever.'

'Come,' Barbara commanded. 'We're heading for the lower levels.'

'What about the others?' Ella asked, worried about her friends.

'They'll hold the line as long as they can,' Barbara said. 'We must get you to safety, Ella.'

Andrew stepped forward. 'I'll stay and help them. You protect my daughter.'

'No, Dad—' Ella started, but he cut her off.

'Ella, this is bigger than any of us. If the Institute gets you, it's over.'

Ella swallowed hard, nodding. 'Be careful.'

Andrew gave her a reassuring smile before turning and running toward the entrance, where the sound of battle intensified.

Barbara grabbed Ella's arm. 'Let's go.' She led them down a narrow passage, moving quickly despite the tremors that shook the place with each distant explosion. Lyssa and Gemma followed, checking for any sign of danger.

They ran through the darkened corridors. The weight of their predicament bore down on Ella as they journeyed further into the pyramid, her thoughts swirling frantically. The relics they'd hidden were their only chance at defeating The Soulless, but now the Institute was closing in on them, relentless in its pursuit of power.

Barbara stopped as they reached a small chamber far below the main level. She turned to face them, her eyes filled with urgency. 'We can't let them find us.'

Ella nodded. 'What's the plan?'

'We'll defend this position,' Barbara declared. 'Whatever it takes.'

'You should take Ella and her mother and get them safe,' Lyssa said. 'It's her they want.'

'And what would you do, child?' Barbara asked.

'Give me the Staff of Souls, and I'll hold them back.'

'No,' Ella replied.

'It's the only way,' Lyssa said. 'There must be another exit somewhere. Find it and get safe.'

Barbara shook her head. 'I'll do it.'

'The energy in the Staff isn't endless,' Lyssa said. 'It will run out soon, taking hours to recharge. We'll all be captured if we stay here.'

Barbara considered this. 'If we can escape, we might be able to find Gisela to get off the island.'

Ella scowled. 'We can't leave the others behind. I won't do it.'

Gemma Finn grabbed her daughter's hand. 'They're fighting for you, love. If the Institute catches you, they'll experiment on you like they do with Elementals. We can't let that happen.'

Ella wanted to scream. 'We must go back for the Book of All Life. I can use that to bring more Elementals here to help us.'

'You might get them killed, Ella,' her mother said.

She knew it was true, pain echoing through her.

Ella didn't know what to do as Barbara handed Lyssa the Staff.

That's when an explosion rattled the room, and everything went dark.

Chapter 22

Revelations

A throbbing, painful electric current swept through Ella as someone dragged her along the ground. Dust swirled over her face, thrusting up her nose and into her mouth. She coughed as her body hit small stones and moved through muddy puddles.

Then the movement stopped, and she opened her eyes, looking up at the vast, blue nothing. Every part of her ached, and she wanted to sleep, but Ella knew she couldn't rest. Something buzzed in her ears as she thrust her hands into the dirt, trying to push herself up, but there was no strength in her arms, and she collapsed.

Ella stared into the sky, seeing it wasn't empty anymore. Tiny dark dots whizzed around, coming closer. Were they making the noises in her head?

She considered the question, realising they were helicopters when strong hands dragged her up, gripping her so she couldn't move.

'Well, at least one of you survived.'

Ella recognised the voice but was unable to place it. Her vision was blurred, and she tasted blood in her mouth.

Where were her parents? What had happened to the others?

'Who...?' she said.

A shadowy figure approached as her eyesight returned to normal.

'Am I that unremarkable, Ms Finn?'

She struggled in the soldier's grip and stared at someone Ella had hoped never to see again. 'Director Black?'

He peered beyond Ella, speaking to somebody behind her. 'Check everywhere for the rest.' Then he turned his focus to her. 'What happened in there, Ms Finn?'

She coughed, spitting into the dirt. 'You blew up the pyramid, you lunatic.'

Black shook his head. 'No, that wasn't us. We were just about to apprehend the traitor Venus and her gang of monsters when the ceiling collapsed. Luckily, most of my people got out in time. Then we found you here. There is no sign of the others yet.'

Ella's head dropped. 'No. No. No.' Her heart ached as she looked up. 'Who dragged me outside?'

He shrugged. 'It wasn't us, though I'm glad somebody did.' His smile irritated her. 'Where is that magical book of yours?'

Ella's body screamed in pain while her mind howled in agony. But at least Black and the Institute hadn't got their dirty hands on the Book of All Life and the other artefacts.

'My parents have it,' she lied. 'You have to search for them and the others.'

He laughed. 'You're giving the orders now?'

She went limp in the soldier's grip, hanging like a drunken puppet. 'Please, I'll do anything.'

Black moved closer, reaching out to touch her cheek. She didn't have the strength to flinch. 'Of course you will.

Maybe we won't need that book. You have some of this magical Light stored inside you, right?'

Yes, she did, even though she hadn't felt its power since arriving on the island. She dug deep within herself, using her mind to search for the Light, going deeper than she'd ever done before, to the furthest parts of her, seeking the thing she knew could save them all.

But there was nothing.

Whatever she'd had, that link with her ancestor, the Goddess Pandora, was long gone. Ella had known it all along, but desperation had made her try one last time.

'The others must be trapped inside, Director,' a man said as he approached Black with two more armed Institute soldiers.

Black stood away from Ella. 'Never mind. Get a recovery team here. Restrain the girl and put her on my copter.' He grinned at her. 'We'll have a long chat on the way back.'

Ella struggled in the soldier's grip, but escaping was impossible.

'Let her go,' a familiar voice commanded.

She twisted her head to see a bloodied Seraphina stumbling towards them.

Gideon Black didn't move. 'Ah, the witch. I don't think we've had a monster like you at the Institute. I'll enjoy watching our scientists studying you.'

Seraphina raised a trembling hand. 'I can fry you like a pig, little man.'

'Really?' he replied as his soldiers aimed their weapons at Seraphina. 'Go on then.'

Seraphina's legs buckled, and she dropped to her knees. Blood dripped from her forehead and mouth as Ella saw the metal shard sticking out of her arm.

'I'm sorry, Ella,' Seraphina said. 'I couldn't save them.'

Director Black laughed. 'Of course you couldn't, witch. You're a monster. And monsters will never defeat humans.'

'Oh, that's debatable,' a female voice declared.

Ella twisted again, but failed to see who'd spoken. Was it Peg? Callisto? Kitty?

'Switch to night vision,' the tallest soldier commanded.

They did, including the one holding her. With only one hand gripping her, Ella wriggled free from his grasp and ran to Seraphina.

She helped her friend up. 'Do you know who said that?'

'No,' Seraphina answered. 'I don't recognise the voice.'

'Nothing shows up on infrared,' a soldier replied.

'Get more people here,' Black commanded.

'It won't matter,' the invisible voice said.

Ella sensed the panic sweeping through the Institute men.

Then Lyssa appeared out of nothing, holding the Staff of Souls with Ella's bag of relics over her shoulder.

'Are you another monster, child?' Black asked.

'You could say that,' Lyssa answered.

She raised the Staff, and a fierce green light burst from it, slicing Black in half. His body fell in two bits as the soldiers opened fire. Ella froze on the spot as the bullets reached her and then stopped in mid-air before falling to the ground. Lyssa's response was to melt the soldiers with emerald flame. Their screams scorched Ella's ears.

Ella bent over and threw up, pain shooting through her chest. She wiped the vomit from her lips and looked at Lyssa. 'You didn't need to kill them.'

Lyssa's grin was inhuman. 'Didn't I?'

'Where are our friends?' Seraphina asked.

Lyssa shrugged. 'Don't know, don't care.'

Realisation seeped into Ella. 'You're not human.'

'Well, aren't you the clever one?' Lyssa said.

Before Ella could reply, more soldiers came running, at least ten of them. Lyssa waved the Staff at them, and they vanished.

'Stop it!' Ella shouted.

Lyssa removed the bag from her shoulder and placed it on the ground. 'Why? These people killed your family. They murdered your friends. They would have imprisoned you and tortured me.'

Ella bit into her top lip. 'My Mum and Dad are not dead.'

'Maybe,' Lyssa answered. 'I didn't look for them, being too busy retrieving this from your little hiding place.'

'What are you?' Seraphina asked.

Lyssa laughed. 'So, now we get to the nitty-gritty. This body, my dear witch, is a conduit for greatness.'

'You're helping The Soulless,' Ella whispered.

'Or she's one of them,' Seraphina added.

'*Them?*' Lyssa said. 'There is no *them*, children. There is only One, as you will soon see.'

Ella swallowed the blood in her mouth. 'Didn't thousands of The Soulless invade Earth in the distant past?'

Lyssa shook her head. 'The Soulless are one entity, but we, they, them, it, can send parts of ourselves into other living things. Like I, they, them, we, it, did with this girl.' Darkness filled her eyes. 'For countless millenniums, we hungered in this vessel, the only part left behind when the humans and Elementals forced me from this realm. This island has been my home for longer than I can remember. Even in this debilitated state, I invaded the minds of the humans here, forcing them to build the pyramid and construct the rune stones inside. Of course I fed on them after. But still, I was imprisoned here.' She smiled at Seraphina. 'And then you arrived with your Elementals. I would never have been strong enough to manipulate you, to get into your mind and speak through you, but you weakened yourself by placing the barrier around this island. Everything was child's play for me after that.' She glanced at Gideon Black's body parts. 'The humans were an unexpected distraction, but nothing more than that.'

Ella peered at her backpack near Lyssa's feet. 'You manipulated us all to retrieve those artefacts. Why?'

'Why? Tell her, witch.'

Blood dripped from Seraphina's fingers. 'She needs them to connect Earth to the realm where the rest of her – most of her – lives.'

'Yes,' Lyssa said. 'And for the first time in an eternity, I will be whole again.' She reached into the bag and removed the Book of All Life. 'This was an unexpected bonus. So thank you.'

'What will you do with it?' Ella asked.

'It's simple, child. It will help me bring Elementals here, and I shall feed on them, consuming all their Light as I enslave humanity to my will.'

Seraphina leapt at Lyssa, who swatted her aside. Seraphina hit a tree and groaned, rolling into the grass. Ella watched the other girl – who wasn't a girl – and thought of her options. She couldn't fight her way out, worried about what had happened to her parents and friends.

'Is there any humanity left in you, Lyssa?'

Lyssa stepped closer to Ella. 'Oh, no. I drained the soul from this human long ago, just like I'm about to do with you, Ella Finn.'

Ella held her breath, ready to throw herself at the creature in human form.

That's when she smelt water in the air. She saw a large, dark cloud descending from the sky. Lyssa also saw it, raising the Staff of Souls to destroy it.

But it burst apart, revealing Peg and Delf in the middle, riding the crest of a wave. They leapt from it as the water crashed into Lyssa, knocking her off her feet. The Staff tumbled from her hand, rolling inches away as the liquid flowed through the grass. Lyssa reached for it before Ella did, about to grab it, when Ella heard the hooves racing towards them. She looked up to see Veronica and Catherine on Agrius. Cat leant down and grabbed the Staff before Lyssa could as Agrius rode through the water. Kitty and Callisto rushed out of the trees, pinning Lyssa to the ground.

Ella's heart raced as she saw her mother and father rushing towards her.

'Are you okay?' Gemma Finn asked as she hugged her daughter.

'Yes,' Ella answered as her dad gripped her hands.

Seraphina staggered to her feet, coughing blood. 'Get the bag. We need the relics to exile the girl.'

Veronica and Catherine dismounted from Agrius. 'Can't we use the Staff to kill her?' Veronica asked.

Seraphina shook her head. 'The Soulless cannot die. All we can do is imprison or banish it.'

'There's been enough killing,' Ella declared, moving towards her backpack.

Then Lyssa roared, sending Kitty and Callisto flying off her. She jumped to her feet, grinning at Ella. 'There's plenty of killing still to come, child. Perhaps I'll start with your parents.'

Ella froze.

Chapter 23

The End

Lyssa's grin was a twisted mask of cruelty as she raised her hand, dark energy coalescing around her fingers. Ella's heart raced as she saw the black tendrils reaching for her parents. She couldn't let it happen. Not again. Not after everything.

'No!' Ella screamed, sprinting forward as the others scrambled to stop Lyssa.

Her feet dug into the earth as she lunged for the Staff of Souls. But Lyssa's power lashed out before she could reach it, throwing her down. The wind was knocked from Ella's lungs as she skidded across the wet grass, mud caking her clothes.

'Ella!' her mother cried, but Lyssa's laughter drowned out Gemma Finn's voice.

'Your Light is flickering, girl,' Lyssa mocked, her form seeming to darken as her power grew. 'You're nothing compared to me!'

Ella tried to get up, but her muscles screamed in agony. Every bone in her body howled like it was on fire. She gasped for air, the taste of blood heavy in her mouth. Her mind scrambled for a solution, but the power she once had —the connection to the Light—felt distant, unreachable.

Lyssa raised her hands, pulling at the force around her as her shadow expanded across the forest. 'Watch as I drain the life from those you love.'

But as the static in the air thickened, Ella saw something —a shimmer of gold, faint but growing brighter. It was the energy from the Staff in Catherine's grasp.

'Use it, Cat!' Veronica shouted, drawing a blade and stepping between Lyssa and Ella's parents.

Catherine looked uncertain, gripping the Staff tighter as Lyssa's dark presence crushed the surrounding air. But the longer she held it, the more the light grew, fighting back against Lyssa's darkness.

'That won't stop me, girl,' Lyssa hissed at Catherine. 'You're too weak to wield it properly.'

Catherine's face twisted with fear, but she didn't release her grip. She nodded to Ella, her eyes fierce. 'I don't need to stop you,' Catherine muttered. 'I only have to delay you.'

Catherine struck the earth with the Staff, and a shock-wave of golden radiance rippled outward. Lyssa snarled in fury as the light clashed with her dark energy, halting her attack on Ella's parents.

'Keep her off balance!' Delf shouted. He and Peg stood side by side, their combined Elemental power surging through the ground and water, pushing Lyssa further back. The dark force around her wavered, but only for a second.

'You can't keep me away forever!' Lyssa screamed, fighting against their powers.

Seraphina, battered but unrelenting, staggered toward Ella. 'We need the relics,' she gasped. 'Without them, we can't finish this.'

Ella crawled towards her bag, hands shaking as she dug

through the soaked fabric. Her fingers brushed against the cold, ancient objects inside: the Eye of the Forgotten, the Warden of Souls heart, and the Book of the Dead. But as she pulled them free, the ground trembled.

The island was collapsing.

The tremors came without warning, rumbling deep from beneath the earth. They started as faint quakes but grew in intensity. Cracking stone echoed across the battlefield as the earth split open.

'Move!' Agrius bellowed, leaping aside as a fissure tore through the ground.

Water surged into the cracks, flooding the land. The ocean was reclaiming the island. The pyramid's destruction had destabilised the foundation of the place, and it was sinking—threatening to drag them all into the depths.

'We have to get off this island!' Veronica screamed, her voice hardly audible over the crashing waves.

'No!' Seraphina shouted, her hand grasping Ella's shoulder. 'If we leave now, Lyssa wins. She'll take the relics and open the portal. We finish this here.'

Unfazed by the surrounding chaos, Lyssa stretched out her hands again. 'You won't be leaving. None of you will,' she sneered as dark wisps snaked toward Ella.

Ella barely had time to react as she clutched the artefacts. The world blurred with motion—waves crashing, soldiers shouting, her family and friends locked in desperate combat with a force far beyond anything they'd ever faced.

Lyssa's tendrils of shadow shot forward, wrapping around Ella's wrist, the cold, dark energy burning through her skin like acid. The ocean's roar muffled her scream as the island crumbled beneath them. The earth shifted, sending everyone staggering. Vast chunks of the earth fell into the sea, swallowed by the murky waters.

Veronica, Peg, Delf, Kitty, and Callisto were all locked in battle with Lyssa, their efforts just keeping her at bay. Catherine and Seraphina tried to hold their ground, but they were faltering. The island was coming apart faster than they could fight. Andrew and Gemma Finn attempted to help their daughter.

Ella knew what she had to do. She had to finish it.

Through the chaos, Ella's mind was clear. She looked at her friends, her parents, and then at Lyssa. She couldn't let Lyssa escape. Not with the relics. Not with the Book of All Life.

'I'm ending this,' she whispered, standing. The ground trembled, but she was steady. She sensed something stirring deep inside her—a flicker of power she hadn't felt since arriving on the island.

Lyssa noticed, her grin faltering. 'You're too late, child. This place is sinking. You'll die here.'

'Maybe,' Ella replied, her voice calm. 'But so will you.'

With a sudden surge of energy, Ella thrust her hand forward. Light burst from her fingers, brighter than it had ever been before. It wasn't the power of the Goddess Pandora, but it was something else—something new.

Lyssa screamed as the Light engulfed her, burning away her dark energy. She staggered away, her form flickering as if struggling to maintain shape.

'No!' Lyssa howled, her voice filled with rage and panic. 'I am eternal! I cannot be destroyed!'

But Ella didn't stop. She poured everything into that moment, pushing Lyssa back further as the Light consumed her. Around them, the island crumbled faster. Gigantic waves surged onto the land, swallowing trees and rocks and engulfing the remains of the pyramid. The ocean was rising, and soon, nothing would be left.

'Ella!' Seraphina shouted. 'We have to go! Now!'

But Ella didn't move. She focused on Lyssa, who was barely holding her form together, her once-confident smirk replaced by a look of pure terror.

'You can't win,' Lyssa hissed, her voice trembling. 'You'll die here too.'

'Maybe,' Ella said. 'But you won't leave.'

With a final burst of Light, Ella unleashed everything. The power surged through her, through the relics, and into Lyssa. The creature let out one last agonised scream as her form shattered into nothingness.

Lyssa was gone.

The victory was short-lived. As soon as Lyssa vanished, the island crumbled. The ground gave way, and everyone scrambled to stay above the water, but it was useless.

'We're going under!' Veronica shouted as she helped Peg onto Agrius's back. Delf pulled Seraphina to safety while Catherine clung to the Staff, her eyes wide with terror. Peg tried to use her powers to calm the ocean, but it was too strong.

Ella stood alone, staring at the sea as it surged toward her.

'Ella!' her mother cried, reaching for her.

But it was too late.

The island sank into the water, and Ella vanished beneath the waves with the relics still clutched in her hands.

Chapter 24

Epilogue

The ocean churned, and Ella's family and friends fought for their lives on the sinking island.

Ella and the relics were gone, swallowed by the sea.

Yet, in the depths of the ocean, something stirred.

The Light had not faded completely.

As the water churned around the sinking island, a faint glow pulsed beneath the surface.

The story wasn't over.

Thank You!

Thank you, dear reader for purchasing this book.

Many thanks to my wonderful wife for all her support and patience.

Editor & proofreader: Karina Gallagher

Cover design by James, GoOnWrite.com